Writer and Artist
MIRKA ANDOLFO

Colorist
SIMON TESSUTO

Letterer
FABIO AMELIA

Editor
CRISTIAN POSOCCO

Associate Editor
DAVIDE G.G. CACI

Logo & Book Design
FABRIZIO VERROCCHI

Localization
STEVE ORLANDO

Cover Artist
MIRKA ANDOLFO

MIRKA ANDOLFO'S SWEET PAPRIKA, VOL. 1 TP. First printing. February 2022. Published by Image Comics, Inc. Office of publication: PO BOX 14457, Portland, OR 97293. Sweet Paprika, created by Mirka Andolfo. © 2022 Andolfo, Arancia Studio s.n.c. All rights reserved. Contains material originally published in single magazine form as MIRKA ANDOLFO'S SWEET PAPRIKA #1-6. "Sweet Paprika," its logos, and the likenesses of all characters herein are trademarks of Mirka Andolfo, Arancia Studio s.n.c., unless otherwise noted. "Image" and the Image Comics logos are registered trademarks of Image Comics, Inc. No part of this publication may be reproduced or transmitted, in any form or by any means (except for short excerpts for journalistic or review purposes), without the express written permission of Mirka Andolfo, Arancia Studio s.n.c. or Image Comics, Inc. All names, characters, events, and locales in this publication are entirely fictional. Any resemblance to actual persons (living or dead), events, or places, without satirical intent, is coincidental. Printed in Canada. For international rights, contact: licensing@aranciastudio.com. ISBN: 978-1-5343-2104-5.

AranciaStudio

OH, I WONDER WHO COULD BE AT THE DOOR...
MR. IMP...IS IT REALLY YOU?
MS. IMP! I JUST HAVE TO TALK TO YOU, I...
I LOVE YOU!
YOU! YOU'RE THE ONLY DEVIL MY HEART BEATS FOR! MARRY ME!
YES, YES, YES, IMP! LET'S GET MARRIED. HERE AND NOW!
I CAN SEE IT NOW! WE'LL HAVE A HOUSE, TEN CARS...
...ONE DOG, THREE CATS, AND SO MANY...
...CHILDREEEN!
WHAT ARE YOU DOING, PAPRIKA?!

NOTHING! I MEAN, THEY WERE JUST, WELL...
COME ON, ARTEMISIO! IT'S JUST A GAME.
MY POINTY HORNS IT'S JUST A GAME, PEPPER! IT'S ALWAYS JUST A GAME...
...UNTIL YOU'RE DROPPING OUT OF MIDDLE SCHOOL DUE TO PREGNANCY!
COULDN'T SHE PLAY MORE INTELLIGENT GAMES?
SHE'S NOT PLAYING WITH DOLLS FOR HER BRAIN, PAPRIKA'S JUST CURIOUS ABOUT SE--
DO NOT SAY THAT WORD!
NOW WE'RE BANNING EVEN THE WORD?
THERE'S THAT ATTITUDE OF YOURS AGAIN, YOU'RE ALWAYS TALKING ABOUT THIS IN FRONT OF HER, THAT'S WHY SHE'S, YOU KNOW...
...LIKE THAT!

CHAPTER 1

MY LIFE DOESN'T STOP AT THE OFFICE DOOR!

INFERNUM PRESS
BURNET
SPICE IT UP!
AS OF TODAY, INFERNUM PRESS IS NOW ONE OF THE WORLD'S TOP PUBLISHERS.
AND IT'S OBVIOUS WHY, I MEAN... 30% OF THE TOP SELLERS COME FROM YOU!
BURNET SPICE IT UP!
30%... THAT'S NO SMALL THING!
AND YOUR FLAGSHIP BOOK ACCOUNTS FOR 10% OF WORLDWIDE SALES ALONE!
DON'T DENY IT... YOU'RE A TREND!
INFERNUM PRESS
THIS IS YOUR MOMENT. YOUR NAME'S ON EVERYONE'S LIPS...SO LET'S OPEN THOSE LIPS WITH A NEW, WONDERFUL LOGO!
SOMETHING RESPECTFUL OF THE ORIGINAL ONE...BUT YOUNG, HIP AND FLY.

I'M TELLING YOU, WITH MY RAD, TRENDY AGENCY...YOU WON'T HAVE TO WORRY ABOUT CONNECTING WITH THE YOUTH.
INFERNUM
WE'VE GOT IT DOWN TO A SCIENCE. WE VERTICALIZE OUR SYSTEMS, WITH INTEGRATED OBLONG S.E.O. PHRASEOLOGY, WHILE OFFERING LATERAL CONTENT SUPPORT, AND...
...OH, MY COFFEE. FINALLY! HOT AS HELL, RIGHT?
GUUULP
...WHAT... IS THIS...?

YOU! WHAT DO YOU HAVE TO SAY FOR YOURSELF? THE OTHER SECRETARY SAID IT'D BE FIVE MINUTES. NOW IT'S TEN...AND IT'S COLD.
ARE YOU EMBARRASSED? YOU SHOULD BE, YOUNG LADY, BECAUSE YOU NEED TO SHAPE UP!
...
DID YOU AT LEAST USE SOME LUKEWARM MILK...ANYTHING TO COMBAT THIS ARCTIC BEVERAGE YOU'VE SERVED ME?
TLAK
WHA-WHAT IS HE DOING?!
CRASH
GNNNN
SIGH SIGH

RATTLE RATTLE
THE DEMON SAINT
MR EVIL
WHAT? THIS IS SUPPOSED TO BE MINE, ISN'T IT? WAS ANYONE ELSE WAITING FOR COFFEE?
SHHHHHH
YOU KNOW...I NEVER TAKE MILK IN MY COFFEE...
BUT IT SEEMS MY FOOLISH ASSISTANT FORGOT TO ADD MY SPECIALLY REFINED MADAGASCAR ANISE SUGAR...
!
...GO AND FIX IT! NOW, YOU USELESS PIECE OF MUD!
PSSST... DON'T TRY TO ARGUE...JUST DO IT!

* CHIEF CREATIVE OFFICER.

I MADE INFERNUM PRESS WHAT IT IS TODAY.
...IF I CATCH YOU CHATTING WITH YOUR BOYFRIEND AT WORK AGAIN, I'LL MAKE SURE HE'S THE ONLY THING YOU GET FOR CHRISTMAS.
THAT'S EXACTLY WHY I CAN'T LET MY GUARD DOWN.
I EXPECT FROM OTHERS ONLY WHAT I EXPECT FROM MYSELF. THAT'S ALL.
WELL? GET GOING, CHAMOMILE! I THOUGHT YOU SAID YOU WENT TO COLLEGE!
BECAUSE I AM A YOUNG WOMAN AND A DEVIL IN A WORLD OF DEMONS AND WARRIOR ANGELS, ALL LOCKED IN AN ETERNAL DICK-MEASURING CONTEST.
YOUR GRANDMOTHER'S FUNERAL CAN WAIT! WE NEED TO GO TO PRINT!
OKAY, MAYBE...I AM JUST A LITTLE BIT OF A SUPERBITCH...BUT IT'S FOR THE GOOD OF THE COMPANY, AND AT LEAST I'M SUPER.
THAT SAID, MY WAY OF DOING THINGS...IT'S NOT VERY GOOD FOR MY SOCIAL LIFE.
SHE'S ALWAYS SITTING THERE ALONE...
PEOPLE ARE AFRAID TO EVEN TRY TO TALK TO ME.
MISS PAPRIKA... THE GIRLS AND I WERE GOING TO TRY A NEW PLACE FOR LUNCH. WE THOUGHT MAYBE YOU'D LIKE TO--
BUSY.
HOLY SALAD
BUT THAT'S FINE... I DON'T HAVE TIME FOR THAT SOCIAL NONSENSE.
CHOMP CHOMP

THERE'S SO MUCH MORE I COULD ACHIEVE, AND SOON, IF I PLAY MY CARDS RIGHT.
JUST LIKE WHEN I WENT FROM A SIMPLE EDITOR TO A C.C.O., THANKS TO MY INSIGHT ON OUR CURRENT BEST-SELLER.
SPICE IT UP! JUST EXCEEDED THE SALES OF HELLY PORTER!
NOBODY CAN RESIST YOUR BOOK, BURNET! ESPECIALLY THE WOMEN!
WHAT'S YOUR SECRET?
BURNET
SPICE IT UP!
IT'S NO SECRET, MY DEAR... I AM A PROVOCATEUR... I KNOW THE FEMALE WORLD WELL, AND I KNOW HOW TO TEASE.
BUT EVERY BUBBLE CAN BURST. EVEN IF THINGS KEEP GOING WELL, THERE'LL STILL BE A DOWNTURN EVENTUALLY...
WHICH MEANS I'LL HAVE TO SEE HIS FACE AGAIN... AND I DON'T LOVE THAT!
ANYWAY. THIS IS NO TIME TO LET MYSELF GET DISTRACTED, I--
CHOMP CHOMP
HI HI HI HI HI HI HI HI HI HI HI HI HI
?
HIM AGAIN?!
DILL...

SBRILL
GOOD MORNING, BEAUTIFUL WOMEN!
IT'S THAT FUCKING DELIVERY BOY!
HERE, A SMALL PACKAGE... DELICATE AND CUTE...IT MUST BE YOURS, CLAIRE!
WONDER Devil
HEAVEN EXPRESS
I WONDER IF THOSE STUPID BITCHES KNOW HE'S NOT GUESSING. HE READS THEIR NAMES ON THE LABELS.
WORK HARD
THIS ONE'S SOFT AS YOUR HAIR, HELEN... ♥
VRR
OH...AND THIS ONE? CYLINDRICAL, LONG... VIBRATES...
VRR
IT HAS TO BE YOURS, ANISETTE!
YOU KNOW, WE COULD PLAY THIS GAME A LITTLE LONGER... IF YOU'RE FREE.

HEY! YOU!
ME?
YOU GAVE THAT PACKAGE TO THE WRONG LITTLE ANGEL, YOU BIG SIDE OF BEEF.
I'M THE ONE YOU'RE LOOKING FOR... IS YOUR OFFER STILL VALID?
MY...MY SWEETEST LADY! IF ONLY I WERE A HUNDRED YEARS OLDER, NOT TO MENTION DEAF, BLIND AND LACKING SENSE OF TOUCH OR TASTE...WE'D BE GREAT TOGETHER!
HA HA HA! ♥
THEN COME TO MY PLACE, DILL... ♥
NO, MINE!
HEAVEN EXPRESS
JUST CALM DOWN, GIRLS.
YOU KNOW THE RULES! NO GIRLFRIENDS, NO WIVES...BUT I'LL BE VERY GENEROUS TO THE REST!
NOT TO ME YOU WON'T! GET LOST!
HELLO THERE!
SEE YOU LATER...
WE'VE TALKED ABOUT THIS. STOP BOTHERING MY EMPLOYEES! LEAVE YOUR PACKAGES AT RECEPTION!
IS IT MY FAULT EVERYONE LOVES ME? I HAPPEN TO BE GREAT AT MY JOB!

WOF, WOF!
YOU DON'T HAVE TO GET SO ANGRY, MISS PAPRIKA!
TRY TO RELAX!
WOF!
WOF!
MAYBE YOU COULD TRY TO BECOME FRIENDS WITH THE DILL-DO!
WHAT IS THIS SUPPOSED TO BE, SOME SORT OF KIDS' SHOW?
WOF!
I'M SURE MY OWNER COULD HELP YOU REALLY RELAX...
WOF!
...
YOU'RE... DISGUSTING!
YOU THINK I WOULD EVER ENGAGE IN SUCH A... SUPERFICIAL CARNAL RELATIONSHIP... WITH A DELIVERY BOY?!
WELL...IS THE PROBLEM "DELIVERY BOY" OR "SUPERFICIAL CARNAL RELATIONSHIP"?
BOTH!
WHAT KIND OF A WOMAN DO YOU THINK I AM?
WHAT ARE YOU SO AFRAID OF?
?!

ARE YOUR COWORKERS "THOSE KIND" OF WOMEN? WHY, BECAUSE THEY LIKE TO HAVE FUN?
YOU KNOW, I'VE BEEN COMING HERE FOR YEARS, AND I'VE NEVER SEEN YOU HAVE AN ACTUAL FRIENDSHIP WITH A SINGLE PERSON.
LOOKING AT HOW YOU JUDGE PEOPLE, I CAN'T SAY I'M SURPRISED.
IS THAT RIGHT? AND WHAT DO YOU CALL WHAT YOU'RE DOING NOW?!
I'M JUST SAYING, EVERYONE SHOULD HAVE FRIENDS! EVEN YOU! ♥
IF ONLY YOU WEREN'T AFRAID OF... WHATEVER YOU'RE AFRAID OF. OTHER PEOPLE DON'T BITE!
I DON'T BITE EITHER... UNLESS YOU WANT ME TO... ♥
I'VE GOT PLENTY OF FRIENDS, ASSHOLE! NOT TO MENTION A LONG LINE OF SUITORS WITH REAL JOBS BANGING DOWN MY DOOR! YOU GOT THAT?!
NOT THAT IT'S YOUR BUSINESS, BUT MY LIFE DOESN'T STOP AT THE OFFICE DOOR!
I'M SURE. FUNNY...IF YOU'VE REALLY HAD ALL THESE "SUITORS," I FIGURE YOU WOULDN'T BE SO WORRIED ABOUT PROVING IT. METHINKS SHE DOTH PROTEST TOO MUCH.
SHUT UP!
YOUR OPINION DOESN'T MEAN SHIT...FUCKING CREEP!
ZIIIIN
DON'T WORRY, BEAN...PAPRIKA'S CLEARLY CRAZY ABOUT US! ♥
OKAY, SO, I LIED...

MY LIFE DOES END AT THE OFFICE DOOR. AND AS SOON AS I LEAVE, I'M A LOSER...
I MEAN, LET ME EXPLAIN, MAYBE "LOSER" ISN'T THE RIGHT WORD. IT'S JUST...
I AM DISGUSTINGLY RICH, I HAVE A DREAM APARTMENT OVERLOOKING CENTRAL PARK, AND AN ENVIABLE CAREER. I LOVE MY JOB, I CAN SAFELY SAY "I MADE IT" BY MY STRENGTH ALONE, AND I'M PROUD OF MYSELF FOR THAT. I DESERVE EVERYTHING I HAVE...SO WHAT DO I MEAN BY "LOSER"?
ANSWER: ONLY ME, MY MOTHER (A FEW TIMES), MY FATHER (NOT EVEN A FEW TIMES) AND THE INTERIOR DESIGNER HAVE EVER SEEN MY PLACE. AND I'VE BEEN LIVING HERE FOR A FEW YEARS. IN SHORT, DILL READ ME PERFECTLY. I'VE GOT NO FRIENDS...AND LET'S JUST NOT TALK ABOUT "SUITORS."
IF YOU'RE NOT OUTGOING, IF YOU DON'T HAVE A WILD SOCIAL AND SEX LIFE, PEOPLE SAY YOU'RE A "LOSER."
BUT I'M SORRY... WHAT EXACTLY IS WRONG WITH ANY OF THAT?
I LIKE IT. I DON'T WANT TO CHANGE.
EVEN IF I WANTED TO, I'M TOO BUSY! EVERY SECOND I SPEND AT HOME IS AN OPPORTUNITY LOST. IT'S NOT MY FAULT, THAT'S HOW THE WORLD WORKS!
HMM...GINGER SALAD? DINNER IS SOLVED!
TAP

THAT MORON DILL, THOUGH... HE'S A MASTER AT CREATING OPPORTUNITIES.
AT LEAST THAT'S WHAT I HEAR.
EVERYONE LOVES HIM... WHETHER THEY WANT TO FUCK HIM OR NOT.
FOR THE LOVE OF BEELZEBUB... HOW THE HELL DOES HE DO IT?!
I MEAN, LOOK AT THAT FOOL!
SURE, HE'S PRETTY HOT, BUT HE'S AN IDIOT WITH NO ASPIRATIONS! ALL HE THINKS ABOUT IS PARTYING AND FUCKING!
A LIBIDINOUS PIG, WITH THOSE USELESS PENGUIN WINGS HE USES TO FLUTTER FROM GIRL TO GIRL! AND FOR WHAT?
SEX IS OVERRATED. DOESN'T MATTER IF THERE'S STRINGS OR NOT.
MASTURBATING IS MUCH MORE EFFICIENT.
THE SAME RESULT, OR BETTER, WITH NONE OF THE HASSLE. I MEAN, I'VE BEEN ALONE FOR SEVEN YEARS, WHO KNOWS MY NEEDS BETTER THAN I DO?
DLIN DLO

HELLO, MA'AM...DID SOMEONE ORDER A SALAD?
YES, THANK YOU...
SBRILL
SALAD!
...
IS EVERY DELIVERY BOY IN THIS WORLD AN ASPIRING MODEL?! IT'S FINE. IT'S FINE...HE'S JUST HERE TO SERVE ME...I MEAN SERVE ME MY DINNER.
KEEP THE CHANGE.
THANK YOU! AND--AND SORRY IF THIS IS WEIRD, BUT...
...IT'S PRETTY RARE TO SEE GIRLS WITH SUCH BEAUTIFUL EYES WHILE I'M WORKING...AND, AND I...
I'VE GOT TO TAKE MY SHOT WHILE I CAN...
WAIT...WHAT'S HAPPENING?
COULD WE SWAP NUMBERS?

ANF!
AH...
ANF!
ANF!
ANF!
ANF!
ANF!
ANF!
ANF!
NNNNNH!
ANF!
UGH... YOU FEEL SO GOOD.
ANF!
WELL... AM I THE "DILL-DO" OR AM I?

WEIRD... THE GLASSES GO ON FIRST? BEFORE THE CLOTHES? NOT THAT I'M COMPLAINING...
I FEEL NAKED WITHOUT THEM!
IS THERE A SECOND SUPERPOWER YOU'RE HIDING BESIDES WHAT'S BETWEEN YOUR LEGS? HEAT VISION MAYBE?
AS MUCH AS I LIKE GETTING YOU HOT, I'D PREFER X-RAY VISION...BUT NO, I JUST LIKE THE MYSTERY.
LIKE I SAID, WEIRD...
...BUT THAT'S WHAT MAKES YOU...
INTERESTING!
THAT'S WHAT EVERYONE SAYS...WHAT ARE YOU UP TO NOW? IT'S STILL EARLY.
ME? NOT SURE YET. WHY...YOU GOT IDEAS?
ZZZ...
I THINK A NEW BURGER PLACE OPENED UP AROUND THE CORNER, SUPPOSED TO BE GREAT.
WE COULD GET SOME FRIES, TALK ABOUT MY MEAT...
CHAD
WELL, HEY... ACTUALLY, I'M ON A DIET...
THEN LET'S FIND ANOTHER PLACE!
...AND I HAVE TO GET UP EARLY! SORRY!
"NO PROBLEM. MAYBE I SHOULD HEAD HOME TOO..."

MAYBE WE COULD GET A **COFFEE?** AND THEN...WHO **KNOWS?**
SBAM
SO...I LIED. **AGAIN!** I **DO** GET SUITORS, I JUST **AVOID** THEM LIKE THE PLAGUE!
WORK OR HOME...FASHION OR PAJAMAS... PERFECT HAIR OR LAZY BRAIDS...THINGS CHANGE, BUT ONE FACT REMAINS THE SAME. PAPRIKA... THE **LOSER**.
I CAN'T CONNECT WITH ANYONE, INSIDE THE OFFICE OR OUT. TO ME, OTHER PEOPLE ARE THERE TO TAKE ORDERS. OR BE SCOLDED. BUT THE TRUTH IS...THAT'S ALL I KNOW. I DON'T **ALWAYS** WANT TO BE THE BAD GUY.
MAYBE I SAID IT FITS ME, BUT THAT'S NOT TRUE. IT **DOESN'T** SUIT ME. I JUST CAN'T HELP IT. I'D LIKE TO OPEN UP TO OTHERS, TO TAKE CHANCES, BUT I CAN'T. **SOMETHING IS BLOCKING ME!** MAYBE I'M TOO INTROVERTED?! OR MAYBE...
...I'M AFRAID OF...OF...WELL, I WON'T BORE YOU FURTHE WITH THE DETAILS.

STILL...IF I OVERCOME THIS "BLOCK"...WHO KNOWS WHAT I COULD DO?
THAT CUTE DEVIL, MAYBE...WHAT WOULD'VE BEEN SO BAD ABOUT HIM?
"WHY DON'T YOU COME IN, AND I'LL MAKE SOME COFFEE RIGHT NOW?"
THERE'S NOTHING WRONG WITH FANTASIZING... JUST A LITTLE BIT!
NOBODY WOULD JUDGE, RIGHT?
OH, PAPRIKA...!
ANF!
MISSIONARY?! WITH YOUR SOCKS STILL ON...WHAT A CONSTRAINT, SO KINKY! IT'S SO BDSM!
YOU'RE SUCH A LUSTY DEVIL!
ANF!
ANF!
ANF!
ANF!
ANF!
NNNHHHHHHHHH! I KNOOOOHHHHH!

ANF!
ANF!
I'LL... I'LL DO WHATEVER YOU WANT, MY SWEET PAPRIKA!
AAAWWWW! ♥
LIKE...LIKE COULD YOU SUCK MY TITS, FOR EXAMPLE? ♥
ANF!
JUST AS I THOUGHT, GIRL! YOU DID END UP A DEGENERATE!
DAD?!
GNAK
THIS IS WHY YOU CANCELED YOUR WEDDING AND MADE THAT RESPECTABLE MAN YOUR EX?
FOR A LIFE OF TIT-SUCKING?!
EVERY DAMN TIME. WELL...

"...THERE'S ALWAYS TOMORROW TO CUM."
NOTHING BETTER THAN WORKING IN BED... JUST TO GET STUFF OFF MY MIND!
THIS IS HOW YOU USE A NICE KING-SIZE BED: SLEEP AND GETTING COZY WITH A LAPTOP. ♥
CRACK
OHHH, YES!
11:00 PM
BY THE WAY, REMEMBER THAT "CAREER ADVANCEMENT" I MENTIONED?
IT'S NOT PUBLIC YET, BUT...WE'RE ABOUT TO SIGN A CONTRACT TO MAKE SPICE IT UP! INTO A MOVIE.
ON "SPICE IT UP" MOVIE PROJECT
[redacted]
Carissimo, eccoci qui!
Siamo molto eccitati all'idea di iniziare quest'avventura e
poi SCEMO chi LEGGE ma torniamo a noi... Mirka è scema
SOON, WE'LL BE MEETING WITH FILM EXECUTIVES, AND IF EVERYTHING GOES WELL, IT WILL BE A FIRST FOR INFERNUM PRESS... I'M SO EXCITED!
♪ QUESTA È UNA STATION WAGON, LO SAI CHE COSTA ASSAJE...? ♫
?!
MOM? AT THIS HOUR?
MOMMY! I WAS SLEEPING, OKAY? I SWEAR! I QUIT WORKING HOURS AGO, I MEAN IT!

WAIT, WHAT? I'LL BE RIGHT THERE! I'M COMING!
OH, DAD...

CHAPTER 2

WITH YOUR HEAD HELD HIGH!

COME ON, YOU COULD JOIN ME ON MY BIKE...WE COULD HIT THE BEACH, WATCH THE SUN GO DOWN AND THEN, MAYBE, THE TWO OF US, WE COULD...
MHHH... WHAT? ♥
WE CAN DO WHATEVER YOU WANT, BABE. I'LL MAKE YOUR EVERY WISH COME TRUE... ESPECIALLY THE DIRTY ONES. AHR AHR!
HEAVEN'S EXPRESS
I'M TEMPTED, FOR SURE... BUT I CAN BE PRETTY DEMANDING, YOU KNOW?
YOU SURE YOU'VE STILL GOT IT, PICKLE?
SURE I'M SURE! I'M ONLY A FEW YEARS OLDER THAN YOU, BABE.
"A FEW"?
OKAY, OKAY! A FEW DECADES, MAYBE. BUT SO WHAT?
DOUBLE THE YEARS, DOUBLE THE EXPERIENCE... AND DOUBLE THE PLEASURE. I MEAN, AT MY AGE, YOU COULD CALL ME...
DADDY!

DILL, WHAT THE-- AGAIN WITH THE SURPRISE HUGS?!
SURPRISE! IT'S TIME TO RECEIVE YOUR AFFECTION! ♥
HEAVEN'S
"DADDY"? IS THIS... SOME KIND OF KINK OF YOURS?
HEAVEN'S EXPRESS
WHAT? NO! HE IS MY DADDY, LIKE, LITERALLY!
ADOPTED DAD... MAKE IT CLEAR, DILL!
AND UNLIKE MY ADOPTED DAD, MY PROSTATE WORKS FINE!
CALL ME! ♥
I TOLD YOU A THOUSAND TIMES...
HEAVEN'S EXPRESS
...DON'T CALL ME DADDY WHEN I'M ON THE PROWL! AND STOP STEALING MY CHICKS!
BUT YOU ARE MY DADDY, WHAT ELSE WOULD I CALL YOU?
AND IF YOU CAN'T SEAL THE DEAL, WHY SHOULDN'T I MAKE A MOVE?
BIG WINGS IS BACK IN TOWN
YOU'VE ALWAYS BEEN UNGRATEFUL!
YOU KNOW HOW HARD IT IS OUT THERE FOR A THICK SINGLE GUY MY AGE? AND THAT'S WITHOUT HIS SON STEALING THE SHOW WITH HIS MODEL-GOOD-LOOKS.
MAYBE SHOW SOME PITY?
NO.
THEN AT LEAST TRY NOT TO BE SO SINCERE?!
NO.
DAMN IT YOU'RE BREAKI MY HEAR
BIG

A HEART ATTACK.
IT WAS SO SUDDEN.
I DON'T GET IT, MOM... HE ALWAYS SEEMED SO HEALTHY.
PAPRIKA, LOVE...THESE THINGS CAN JUST HAPPEN, WHEN YOU GET OLD...
WE SHOULD ACCEPT IT.
NO...
I CAN'T ACCEPT IT, NOT LIKE THIS.
SOMEWHERE, SOMEONE... SOMETHING HAD HIM SO WORRIED, HE HAD A HEART ATTACK. POOR DADDY...

GET WELL
HEY! DON'T YOU KNOW I'M STILL ALIVE?!
...WOULD YOU STOP THIS ITALIAN-AMERICAN DRAMA?!
TAKE CARE
ARTEMISIO, PLEASE...CAN'T YOU SEE HOW HURT PAPRIKA IS?
SHE STAYED UP ALL NIGHT, AND ONLY JUST WENT HOME TO SHOWER AND GET READY FOR WORK!
RIGHT. WORK... DRESSED AS A PROSTITUTE!
BUT THIS... THIS IS MY DOGE & GABBATA TAILLEUR! IT'S FROM THEIR LATEST COLLECTION!
AND YOU STILL HAVEN'T TOLD US WHAT HAPPENED!
DID YOU EAT SOMETHING BAD? WAS IT YOUR NERVES? MAYBE SOMETHING STRESSFUL WITH THE JURY...
OR MAYBE YOU WERE JUST TOO FATIGUED?
WHAT? FATIGUED? I WASN'T DOING ANYTHING UNUSUAL.
ARE YOU SURE?
YE-YES, OF COURSE!
HEY, GRUMPY!
OH...HELLO, BERRY.
HI, SWEETIE!

LET'S GET THE KIDS TO SCHOOL AND HEAD HOME, OKAY?
YES! WE'VE GOT A DATE FOR CUDDLING!
BLEARGH!
BYE! PLEASE...JUST BE SURE TO RELAX, OKAY?
I WAS TALKING TO PAPRIKA.
PFF...LIKE YOU EVEN CARE.
BAH! KISSING LIKE THAT IN FRONT OF THE KIDS? WE WOULD BARELY TOUCH EACH OTHER'S LIPS IF YOU WERE NEARBY.
YOU CAN SEE WHY SOME ANGELS THINK DEVILS ARE DEGENERATES. THEY JUST REINFORCE THE STEREOTYPE.
COME ON, DAD! ARE YOU REALLY STILL JEALOUS, AFTER ALL THESE YEARS?
JEALOUS? ME? NEVER!
THIS IS ABOUT MANNERS! SOMETHING YOU OBVIOUSLY DON'T UNDERSTAND.
AND BY THE WAY, YOU'RE THE ONE WHO SHOULD BE JEALOUS!
ME?! JEALOUS OF WHAT?
YOUR MOTHER REMARRIED. SHE HAD OTHER KIDS, ALL WHILE YOU'RE STILL A SPINSTER!
HERE WE GO AGAIN...KILL ME, PLEASE...
YEAH, YOU'RE RIGHT... I JUST NEED TO FIND THE RIGHT GUY...
YES, OF COURSE. AND HOW DO YOU PLAN TO FIND THE RIGHT GUY WHEN YOU WORK DAY AND NIGHT? NOT TO MENTION...

...YOU INSIST ON KEEPING YOUR NECKLINE SO SINFULLY LOW! I DON'T WANT TO THINK ABOUT WHAT KIND OF MEN YOU ATTRACT. A GOOD MAN WOULD NEVER MARRY SOMEONE SO INTENT ON EXPOSING HER BODY!
YOU LOOK CHEAP!
!
I DON'T KNOW HOW IT HAPPENED, I--I'LL ZIP IT BACK UP!
THE ONE TIME YOU HOOK A SERIOUS PROSPECT...YOU LEFT HIM AT THE THE ALTAR LIKE A FOOL.
NO, PLEASE...NOT THIS, NOT AGAIN!
THERE WAS A MAN OF PRINCIPLES...HE CARED ABOUT YOU! HE HAD CLASS, CULTURE...YOU WOULDN'T HAVE WANTED FOR A THING WITH HIM, YOU COULD'VE QUIT WORKING!
STOP...
YOU'D HAVE BEEN HAPPY RIGHT NOW, YOU'D HAVE HAD KIDS! INSTEAD YOU'RE STRESSED, SAD AND ALONE.
I SHOULDN'T GET ANGRY. IT'S NOT WORTH IT.
HE DOESN'T CARE ABOUT MY CAREER. HE'S OBSESSED WITH A RELATIONSHIP I ENDED SEVEN YEARS AGO...AND HE STILL THINKS HE'S THE ONE, IN HIS UNQUESTIONABLE JUDGMENT, THAT DECIDES WHAT MY PRIORITIES SHOULD BE...
...BUT HE NEVER REALLY KNEW THE MAN I COULDN'T MARRY.
KRIIK
KRIIK

...NOT LIKE I KNEW HIM.
OH, YOUR SHIRT'S A LITTLE OPEN!
WHAT? EHRM... SORRY!
YOU'RE PAPRIKA, RIGHT? YOUR DAD'S THAT FAMOUS ITALIAN LAWYER, RIGHT?
HOW'D YOU KNOW THAT...?
I MEAN, A CUTE GIRL LIKE YOU...DOESN'T GO UNNOTICED.
PLUS, YOUR DAD IS A REAL STAR.
CU-CUTE? ME?
YEAH, YOU...HERE YOU GO, LET ME--
STOP! I'LL DO IT MYSELF!
WHAT...? YOU WANT ME TO PULL OVER?
PULL OVER? NO...SORRY! I'M SORRY! KEEP DRIVING.

I CAN'T TAKE THIS ANYMORE! I CAN'T GO ON!
GLUG
SO THAT'S WHY SHE'S MAKING MY LIFE HELL?
...YOU'RE JUST THE NEWBIE, RUE.
IS IT TOO MUCH TO HOPE FOR A THANK YOU EVERY ONCE IN A WHILE?!
WORK MORE! -PAPRIKA
SHE'S LIKE THIS WITH EVERYONE.
THE BOSS IS JUST...EVIL. BUT GENERALLY, NOT SPECIFICALLY.
YOU GET USED TO IT.
WAY TOO MUCH. I'VE WORKED HERE LONGER THAN MS. PAPRIKA, I KNOW EVERYONE. SHE STILL CALLS ME "GUY."
SHE REMEMBERS YOUR NAME. FOR HER, THAT'S ALMOST KIND. ME? I THINK SHE HATES MEN...
!
BIG WINGS IS BACK IN
WELL, THAT CLEARS THINGS UP: THE MEN IN HER LIFE ARE NOTHING LIKE ME! ♥
...DELIVERY BOYS WHO DO MORE FLIRTING THAN WORK?
YOU'RE ONLY SAYING THAT BECAUSE YOU'RE NOT YET FAMILIAR WITH THE DILL-DO. ♥
ABOUT THAT...YOU GOT ANY PLANS TONIGHT?
I'M HAVING DINNER WITH MY WIFE, CHAMP...WHAT ABOUT YOU?
LET ME GO...
OKAY! MY BAD!
SO, ANYWAY...
WAIT! I THINK I JUST HAD AN IDEA!
CHAMOMILE! MY COAT!
SBRILL

THANK YOU FOR BEING HERE, EVERYONE. OR, MY DEAR UNDERLINGS, SHOULD I SAY...
...ALMOST EVERYONE.
YOUR GREAT DARKNESS, MS. PAPRIKA IS A BIT LATE... OR SO WE'VE BEEN TOLD.
HOW UNFORTUNATE, AND RUDE! AND...BIZARRE. PAPRIKA'S USUALLY THE FIRST TO ARRIVE.
YEAH, WHEN IT'S TIME TO SHOW OFF, SHE'S FIRST IN LINE.
AND THAT'S ADMIRABLE, CONSIDERING HOW LONG IT MUST TAKE TO PUT MAKEUP ON A FACE THAT... PECULIAR. DON'T YOU THINK?
YOU JUST NEED TO TELL ME WHAT KIND OF PLASTER YOU USE, MY DEAR ANISETTE. THAT WOULD SPEED THINGS UP, FOR SURE...
COFF COFF...

CLICK
IF YOU DON'T MIND, LADIES...
TONIGHT, AFTER MONTHS OF NEGOTIATIONS, WE'RE ON THE CUSP OF THE DEAL FOR THE SPICE IT UP! MOVIE.
YOU ALL KNOW HOW MUCH THIS MEANS FOR INFERNUM PRESS. BUT IT WON'T BE EASY.
BURNET, THE BOOK'S AUTHOR, WILL BE INVOLVED, AND HE'LL DO EVERYTHING HE CAN TO MAKE SURE HE GETS THE BIGGEST PIECE OF THIS PIE.
BUT HE'S NOT OUR WORST PROBLEM.
ZA'ATAR, OF PURGATORY PICTURES. HE'S THE REAL DEAL. HE'LL BE EXECUTIVE PRODUCER ON THE ADAPTATION. HE HAD US REVISE THE CONTRACT HUNDREDS OF TIMES IN THE LAST TWO MONTHS.
WHO KNOWS WHAT HE'LL PUT US THROUGH ON THIS DEAL. IF WE DON'T CONTAIN HIM, HE'LL HURT US.
MMH... AND SINCE WE'RE TALKING SWEETS, THAT'S A TREAT I WON'T MIND SNACKING ON! ♥
EENY MEENY, MINY, MOE...WHICH OF THEM DO I WANT TO BLOW? IF THEY WINK AND ASK ME SO, MAYBE BOTH, I WON'T SAY NO!
KEEP IT IN YOUR PANTS, PLEASE.
HAVE YOU SEEN ZA'ATAR?! GET HIM HERE, NOW...AND I'LL MAKE HIM GO DOWN SO DEEP HE'LL NEED SCUBA GEAR!

ENOUGH CHATTER, YOU TWO!
YOU WILL COOPERATE, YOU WILL BE KIND. AND YOU WILL BE VERY...
SBAM
...ACCOMMODATING TO OUR GUESTS.
WELL, THEN. I DIDN'T KNOW YOU WERE SO BOLD, YOUR GREAT DARKNESS.
WHA-WHAT DO YOU MEAN...?
WELL, DON'T GET ME WRONG...
I MEANT THAT I NEED YOU BOTH SHARP AND BRILLIANT TONIGHT. THIS CANNOT BE ANOTHER BORING BUSINESS MEETING. THE DINNER SHOULD BE ELEGANT AND FORMAL, YES...BUT ALSO FRIENDLY.
YOU DON'T WORRY ME, ANISETTE. YOU'RE SOCIAL, AN EXTROVERT. BUT MS. PAPRIKA, YOU ON THE OTHER HAND...
ME?!
IT'S JUST YOU BEING EASILY OVERWHELMED BY ANGER AND ANXIETY. AND THAT SHOULDN'T HAPPEN. DO YOU KNOW WHY?
WH-WHY?
HAVE YOU FORGOTTEN HOW MANY EXCUSES YOU PULLED TO GET OUT OF BEING HERE? I KNOW HOW MUCH THIS BOTHERS YOU, AND I KNOW WHY!
WHAT? NO! IT'S JUST THAT...

BECAUSE YOU'RE THE REASON WE'VE COME THIS FAR! YOU WERE THE ONE THAT GAVE SPICE IT UP! A CHANCE!
TONIGHT, I WANT YOU TO BE CONFIDENT, WITH YOUR HEAD HELD HIGH!
TONIGHT... YOU'RE A DRAGON, GOT IT?
...AB-- ABSOLUTELY!
LET'S GIVE MS. PAPRIKA A ROUND OF APPLAUSE, EVERYONE!
THA-THANK YOU!
CLAP
CLAP
CLAP
CLAP
CLAP
HIS GREAT DARKNESS MIGHT BE SCARY, BUT DEEP DOWN, HE'S GOT A HEART OF GOLD...AND, AS ALWAYS, HE'S RIGHT! I NEED TO BE CONFIDENT!
INFERNUM PRESS
IT DOESN'T MATTER HOW HARD IT'LL BE. I'LL STAY CALM, JUST LIKE HERE AT WORK, AND EVERYTHING WILL BE FINE!
THERE WON'T BE ANY MORE "PAPRIKA THE LOSER"!
HE HE! ♥
THERE'S ABSOLUTELY NOTHING THAT COULD STRESS ME OUT, NO SIR! I'M TOTALLY IN ZEN MODE... ZEN...I'M STAYING ZEN...
UH?! WAIT A SECOND!
CHAMOMILE! WHY ISN'T LUNCH ON MY DESK YET?!
CRACK
!

I'M SORRY, YOUR DEVILISH MAGNIFICENCE, OH POWERFUL LADY BOSS!
I WAS ONLY TRYING TO MAKE SURE THE TEA WAS PRECISELY THE RIGHT TEMPERATURE!
THEN I HOPE YOU BROUGHT GINGER LICORICE!
I'M ALREADY PISSED ABOUT WORKING THROUGH LUNCH!
I AT LEAST NEED SOME GINGER...
450 new messages
STRIZZ
IT'S GOING TO BE A LONG DAY!
PROJECTS TBA!
CALL
I HAVEN'T SLEPT, MY DAD'S DRIVING ME NUTS, AND TONIGHT'S THE MOST IMPORTANT EVENING OF THE YEAR!
IS HAVING LUNCH ON TIME SUDDENLY A LUXURY?
OF COURSE NOT, MA'AM!
GOOD! NOW GET THE HELL OUT OF HERE!
STRIZZ
STRIZZ
STRIZZ
STRIZZ
WELL...I CAN STILL ENJOY MY SOLE MOMENT OF DELIGHT.

BUCKWHEAT BRUSCHETTA WITH ORGANIC TRUFFLE TARTARE, AND ULTRA-EXTRA VIRGIN OLIVE OIL FROM SOUTHWESTERN SICILIAN GROWERS, WITH HINTS OF BALSAMIC VINEGAR, IMPORTED DIRECTLY FROM MODENA ON AN ANCIENT VESSEL.
CALORIES: COUNTLESS... BUT FUCK IT!
FOR MISS PAPRIKA! - Chef
WHO NEEDS FRIENDS WHEN I CAN GET TO ENJOY LITTLE MIRACLES LIKE THIS? OH, ANTI-GOD... I FEEL SO... EXCITED!
I NEED IT INSIDE OF ME, NOW! ♥
OH, YES...I'M GOING TO SWALLOW IT ALL!
SLURP
TOC
TOC
TOC TOC
TOC
TOC
TOC
TOC
DO. NOT. BOTHER. ME.
WELL, IT'S YOUR NAME ON THIS PACKAGE, MS. PAPRIKA. ♥
I'M JUST DOING MY JOB!
UH?
AND WHAT'S THIS? SEEMS DIFFERENT FROM THE BOXES YOU BRING OTHER FOLKS AROUND HERE.

IT IS KIND OF UNUSUAL. IT'S PETITE, CUTE...
FINE PAPER, SMOOTH TO THE TOUCH.
THE KIND THAT SLIPS AWAY THE MORE YOU TRY TO HOLD IT.
HEAVEN'S EXPRESS
IT REMINDS ME OF SOMEONE, MS. PAPRIKA.
IT'S GOT TO BE YOURS!
YOU'RE COMPARING ME TO A BOX?
YOU NEVER ACCEPT MY COMPLIMENTS!
SIGH!
SNFF
AND SPEAKING OF ACCEPTING, HOW ABOUT TONIGHT, WE--
SBAM
I'M WAY TOO BUSY RIGHT NOW. LEAVE IT, I'LL OPEN IT LATER.
THIS BOX IS NOT FROM HEAVEN'S. BUT...
SO...
FRUSH
FRUSH
...WHO THE HELL WOULD SEND IT...?
BURP

UFF, I WANT TO GO HOME...
HEAVEN'S EXPRESS
01
I TOLD HIM NOT TO DRINK ANYTHING FROM THAT VENDING MACHINE.
I USED ITS COFFEE TO CLEAN MY MUFFLER ONE TIME!
IT NEARLY BURNED THROUGH THE THING!
TOILET
HI HI HI!
?

...I DON'T KNOW, MAYBE I SHOULD GET BEAN A NEW HARNESS. BUT THEN AGAIN, SHE'S ALWAYS IN MY ARMS OR HANGING OUT IN MY BAG, SO...
EHM! ♥
SO-SORRY, I'M INTO MULTITASKING, SOMETIMES MY MIND'S ALL OVER THE PLACE AT ONCE.
BUT BELIEVE ME... I'M ENJOYING THIS! ♥
I KNOW... ♥
BUT MAYBE... I WANT YOU TO FOCUS YOURSELF...
...SOMEWHERE MORE SPECIFIC? ♥
IT'LL BE MY PLEASURE! ♥

DOES IT FEEL GOOD?
OH YEAH. DOES IT FEEL GOOD FOR YOU? ♥
SO GOOD... ♥ I WAS JUST THINKING...
ANF!
ANF!
ANF!
AFTER I BRING DADDY BACK HO-HO-HOME...
ME AND YOU...MAYBE WE CAN PICK UP WHERE WE LEFT OFF? ♥
ANF!
...MMH, BRINGING UP YOUR DAD, RIGHT NOW...THAT'S NOT WEIRD AT ALL!
SORRY, YOU'RE RIGHT!
ANF!
OH, YES! YES! ♥
GRE-GREAT, I'LL PICK YOU UP AT...
I WASN'T MOANING ABOUT THAT, SWEETIE! ♥
ANF!
ANF!
ANF!
ANF!
DILL, YOU'RE A =AAAAHN= SWEET GUY.
BUT I THOUGHT...WE BOTH WANTED SOMETHING SIMPLE, NO STRINGS...IF I GOT THAT WRONG...MAYBE WE SHOULD STOP, I DON'T WANT TO HURT YOU...
ANF!
WHAT? NO! I WANTED THE SAME THING! MAYBE...WE SHOULD DO A LITTLE LESS TALKING... YEAH?
I MEAN, I--I'M ALMOST THERE!
ANF!
ANF!
WOAH, ME TOO! I'M ABOUT TO-- ♥
ANF!
KEEP YOUR VOICE DOWN, I DON'T WANT...
ANF!
ANF!

OOOH!
SHHHT!
I KNEW IT!
IT'S ALWAYS THE SAME STORY!
UHHH...
I'M COMING, DADDY! JUST A MINUTE!
Z
LOOK, DON'T BE ANGRY AT ME. I TOLD YOU I WAS GOING TO MAKE A MOVE!
HOW DO YOU EVEN KEEP TRACK OF IT? AND WITH ALL YOUR HOOKUPS AT INFERNUM PRESS, TOO...
Z
COME ON, I HAVEN'T HOOKED UP WITH EVERYONE, NOT YET, AT LEAST! THERE'S STILL THIS LADY WITH GLASSES THAT...
YEAH, ABOUT THAT!
SOMEONE FROM INFERNUM MIGHT'VE SLIPPED A PACKAGE FOR HER INTO OUR PILE WHEN I WASN'T LOOKING...
ZZ
MAYBE SHE HAS A SECRET BOYFRIEND! IT'D SERVE YOU RIGHT!
I DON'T THINK SO. AS A MATTER OF FACT...

I'VE GOT A BAD FEELING ABOUT THIS.
BUT I'M A **GROWN-UP** DEVIL. THE BOSS IS **COUNTING ON ME** AND I WON'T LET HIM DOWN!
THE **PUBLISHER** IS COUNTING ON ME, TOO. **EVERYONE** IS.
AND I AM **CONFIDENT!**
I'M **NOT** THE GIRL I USED TO BE.
I'VE **CHANGED!**
GLOSS
BURGE
SPICE IT UP
THEN **WHY** AM I FEELING... LIKE THIS?
EVERY MINUTE THAT PASSES, I FEEL A **BIGGER WEIGHT** ON MY HEART, HEAVIER AND HEAVIER...

UGHF...
DAMN IT! I'M A HYPOCRITE!
A HYPOCRITE AND A LIAR!
YOU KNOW, PEOPLE THINK I ONLY CARE ABOUT WRITING... BUT I HAVE ANOTHER DREAM. PRACTICING LAW! I COULD BE HAPPY DOING THAT, TOO!
YEAH? SO...I LIKE WRITING, TOO...
YEAH? WHAT GENRE DO YOU LIKE?
...NO-NOTHING... NOTHING TOO PECULIAR! HE HE! ♡
MY FATHER ISN'T THE ONE OBSESSING OVER A RELATIONSHIP THAT DIED YEARS AGO.
HE'S NOT THE ONE ALWAYS THINKING ABOUT MY EX...
IT'S ME, AND MY INABILITY TO LET GO OF THE PAST.

COME ON...I'M CURIOUS, NOW!
I CAN'T RESIST SHY CUTIE DEVILS LIKE YOU...
THEY ALWAYS FIND SOME WAY TO BE SURPRISING...
AND WHAT'S WORSE...
PAPPY!
LONG TIME NO SEE!
...I'M THE ONE WHO BROUGHT THE PAST TO MY DOOR.

CHAPTER 3

YOU DO REMEMBER HOW TO HAVE FUN, RIGHT?

VACATION?!
ARE YOU JOKING, GARI?
NO, ARTEMISIO. IT'S NO JOKE.
LISTEN. THIS STUPID HEART ATTACK KEPT ME OUT OF COURT LONG ENOUGH.
I'M THE MOST RESPECTED AND FEARED JUDGE IN THE COUNTRY. I CAN'T ABANDON THE CASE NOW, AND--
AND YOU'VE ALREADY BEEN PULLED FROM THE CASE.
YOU'VE GOT TO BE JOKING NOW!
IT'S FOR YOUR OWN GOOD.
JUST LOOK AT THE STATE YOU'RE IN.
GIVE ME A BREAK! WE'VE WORKED TOGETHER FOR TWENTY YEARS. I KNOW WHEN YOU'RE SCREWING WITH ME.
YOU DON'T GIVE A DAMN ABOUT MY HEALTH!
WELL, WE'RE ALSO WORRIED ABOUT THIS WHOLE... SITUATION. BUT LOOK AT IT THIS WAY--DON'T YOU MISS ITALY?
A LITTLE TRIP, SOME REST...SOME TIME TO RECHARGE COULD DO WONDERS.
I TOLD YOU! EVERYTHING'S UNDER CONTROL.
ALL THE BETTER REASON TO RELAX, I'D SAY.
BUT IF COMMON SENSE WON'T CONVINCE YOU TO DO THAT...

...MAYBE THINK OF YOUR LOVED ONES?
IF I WERE YOU, I'D WANT TO BE AROUND IF SOMETHING EVER GOES SOUTH.
MH...
MAYBE YOU'RE RIGHT.
SO IT'S SETTLED. AS SOON AS YOUR PLANE LANDS, YOU'LL SEND A NICE POSTCARD TO YOUR EX-WIFE AND DAUGHTER!
I'M C.C.O. OF INFERNUM PRESS. ONE OF THE WORLD'S TOP PUBLISHERS.
YOU KNOW HOW I, A LITTLE PARTHENOPEAN DEVIL, GOT THIS FAR? WITH CALM, WITH REASON, AND...
...WITH A FUCKING TAXI.
YEAH, A TAXI. SOMETHING MY ASSISTANT IS APPARENTLY INCAPABLE OF FINDING.

MISS PAPRIKA...IT'S SATURDAY NIGHT IN MANHATTAN. I'VE CALLED A HUNDRED TAXI COMPANIES BUT...
I WANT TO GO HOME!
YOUR LIFE'S MISSION IS TO MAKE MY LIFE SIMPLER! SO COME GET ME YOURSELF!
WHAT ARE YOU DOING HERE? WORKING OVERTIME LIKE THE REST OF US?
GOT NOTHING BETTER TO DO.
WHAT A WILD LIFE.
BUT MISS PAPRIKA...MY CAR IS STILL BEING REPAIRED FROM AFTER THE LAST TIME WE HAD TO RACE TO GET THAT PURSE FROM LOUIS DEVILON'S LAST COLLECTION...
AH, WELL, SO WORTH IT FOR ME... ♥
SO, LIKE I WAS SAYING...
MOVE! I'M TIRED.
THE NIGHT'S GOING GREAT. OUR NEW BEST-SELLER SPICE IT UP! IS SET TO BE A MOVIE FROM PURGATORY PICTURES.
PAPERS HAVE BEEN SIGNED, PASSIVE-AGGRESSIVE JOKES IGNORED, AND ASSHOLE LAWYERS CONTAINED. IT'S DONE. I'M CONTENT...
TO US!
BUT I WASN'T EXPECTING THESE TROGLODYTES TO WANT TO PARTY AFTERWARDS.
I'M NOT STAYING A MINUTE LONGER THAN I HAVE TO IN A PLACE SO FULL OF PEOPLE BEING...SOCIAL. CAN'T THEY TALK BUSINESS?
I COULD BE BACK IN MY OFFICE, WITH PEOPLE SUFFERING MY EVERY WHIM, OR BACK IN MY APARTMENT, COMPLAINING ABOUT HOW INFERIOR EVERYONE ELSE IS.
SO, TELL ME, BURNET...
DID YOU AND HER REALLY...?

OH YES, BUT IT WAS AGES AGO! A BIT AFTER WE BROKE UP, SHE BECAME THE EDITOR OF SPICE IT UP!. BUT BETWEEN US, YOU KNOW HOW WOMEN GET AROUND ME...
...I DON'T THINK SHE'S TOTALLY OVER ME. PAPRIKA'S SWEET, THE WAY SHE LOOKS AT ME.
HUH?
I THOUGHT SHE LEFT YOU AT THE ALTAR AND BROKE YOUR HEART.
IT SOUNDS LIKE YOU MISUNDERSTOOD THE SITUATION ZA'ATAR!
EITHER WAY, IT WAS FOR THE BEST. SHE WASN'T THE RIGHT WIFE FOR ME, BUT AS AN EDITOR ON THE OTHER HAND...
SO YOU TWO STAYED FRIENDS? IT'S JUST A WORK RELATIONSHIP?
HM.
WELL, I BETTER GO SAY HELLO TO HER... WISH ME LUCK.
IF YOU DON'T MAKE IT BACK, WE'LL SEND THE POLICE TO LOOK FOR YOUR REMAINS.
CAN YOU IMAGINE?
THAT ICY DEVIL LYING IN BED WITH SOMEONE LIKE BURNET?
I DON'T THINK IT WISE TO GOSSIP ABOUT YOUR SUPERIORS WITH SOMEONE YOU BARELY KNOW, MISS ANISETTE...YOU'RE ALSO IN EDITORIAL, RIGHT?
LAMEEEEEE.

!
TING TING
TO SPICE IT UP! AND TO THE GREATEST EDITOR EVER!
I'M C.C.O. NOW. WHAT DO YOU WANT?
I'M... EHRM... CHECKING ON THE OTHERS.
ARE YOU ALWAYS SO DEFENSIVE?
WE BARELY SEE EACH OTHER THESE DAYS, IS SMALL TALK TOO MUCH TO ASK?
TO SEE HOW YOU ARE? WHAT YOU'VE BEEN UP TO?
HOW'S YOUR DAD? I HEARD HE'S SICK...I'M SORRY!
WE WERE SO CLOSE!
YEAH, THAT WAS ONE OF YOUR FEW USEFUL QUALITIES.
YOUR NEEDS ALWAYS CAME BEFORE MINE.
COME ON, PAPPY! SO MAYBE I WAS A LITTLE SELFISH AT THE TIME.
AND MANIPULATIVE, NARCISSISTIC, POSSESSIVE...
OUCH. I KNOW, AND I'M SORRY, BUT WE'RE BOTH DIFFERENT PEOPLE NOW!
LOOK HOW FAR WE'VE GOTTEN WITH STUPID SEXY BOOK. DO YOU REMEMBER WHAT YOU SAID BACK THEN?
I'M PROUD OF WHAT WE ACCOMPLISHED TOGETHER.
AND I WANT YOU TO BE HAPPY...THIS IS YOUR NIGHT TOO!
YOU DO REMEMBER HOW TO HAVE FUN, RIGHT?
HE HE HE!
HE SEEMS SINCERE.
MAYBE I SHOULD LISTEN TO HIM...
HOLDING ON TO ANGER FROM A SEVEN-YEAR-OLD BREAKUP... IS TOTALLY ME.
MAYBE I'M STILL NOT READY TO BE THE PARTY GIRL, BUT HE'S RIGHT, THIS IS MY TIME TO SHINE! I WON'T LET HIM GET ALL THE CREDIT!
WATCH OUT, BOREDOM! ANISETTE TO THE RESCUE!

COME TO THINK OF IT, MY TAXI IS RUNNING LATE...MAYBE THAT'S A SIGN.
WHAT HAVE I BEEN MISSING ALL THIS TIME?
OH, YES... LOOK AT THOSE.
THEY'RE AMAZING, THEY'RE CALLING ME.
WHO AM I TO RESIST SUCH DELICIOUS SNACKS?
MY FATHER HATED THE SINFUL DEVIL STEREOTYPE, ALWAYS TOLD ME TO AVOID TEMPTATION, TO BEHAVE.
WELL...FUCK BEHAVING!
I AM A DEVIL!
AND I AM GOING TO FUCKING INDULGE!
THE LAST 5000-CALORIE MUFFIN BELONGS TO ME!
MAYBE TOMORROW I'LL EVEN SKIP BREAK...
OH, MISS PAPRIKA?
SORRY, I DIDN'T NOTICE YOU THERE.
I HAVEN'T EVEN TOUCHED THE MUFFIN... IT'S YOURS, IF YOU WANT IT.

ZA'ATAR IS A PRODUCER AT PURGATORY PICTURES. HE WAS HARD TO DEAL WITH DURING NEGOTIATIONS.
SOMEONE LESS EDUCATED WOULD SAY HE'S A PAIN IN THE ASS...AND I MIGHT AGREE.
WE ALL WANT THE MOVIE TO SUCCEED. BUT HE WANTS AS MUCH OF THE SUCCESS AS POSSIBLE FOR HIMSELF. AND HE'S VERY CLOSE TO BURNET. IF THAT WASN'T ENOUGH...
NE-NEVERMIND, YOU GOT IT FIRST.
I INSIST, WE CAN SHARE IT!
SERIOUSLY... NO THANK YOU!
...HE IS A DOMINANT BOSS, A WORKAHOLIC, WHO NEVER LEAVES HOME IN ANYTHING BUT A TAILORED SUIT.
IN SHORT... I RESPECT HIM.
AND, ABOVE ALL ELSE, HE REALLY GETS ME HORNY!
YOU SURE? MAYBE JUST A LITTLE BITE?
A BITE?! I WANT IT ALL!
NO, THANK YOU.
I NEED TO STAY CALM. HE IS, AFTER ALL, THE ENEMY.
AND HE'S ONLY BEING POLITE BECAUSE WE'RE EQUALLY POWERFUL.
I'LL JUST GRAB ANOTHER DESSERT AND CALL CHAM.
MAYBE I CAN OFFER YOU A DRINK, THEN?
DAMN, IF ONLY I COULD ACCEPT...
BUT, YOU SEE... I HAVE TO GO...
NEW
PI PI PI
BOSS
Nice.
Accommodating.
GO GIRRRRL!

OH, PICKLE!
DO YOU REALLY WANT TO STAY HERE TONIGHT?
I THOUGHT YOU HAD TO GET UP EARLY.
DON'T WORRY. I'D LOVE TO STAY UP LATE WITH YOU, LOOKING AT THE STARS AND...OTHER THINGS. =HAR! HAR!= IF YOU'D LIKE THAT, OF COURSE.
HEAVEN'S EXPRESS
OH, YOU ARE SO SWEET!
YEAH, BABY! YOU'RE FUN, BEAUTIFUL, AND MOST OF ALL...
...TOO OLD FOR MY SON.
...I HOPE.
SORRY, WHAT?
I MEAN... MY SON DILL WOULD LOVE YOU, I KNOW IT.
ABOUT THAT. I WAS JUST NOTICING...
HEAVEN'S EXPRESS
...THIS RING. DO YOU STILL THINK ABOUT HIS MOTHER?
OF COURSE! SHE'S THE REASON I ADOPTED THAT SWEET KID.
THE RING REMINDS ME THAT SHE'D WANT ME TO BE HAPPY AGAIN, WITH SOMEONE SPECIAL...
OH, PICKLE! DO YOU THINK I COULD BE THAT SOMEONE?
OF COURSE, BABY...
DADDYYY...
CAN I BORROW THE CAR?! I NEED IT TO SAVE A NICE LADY FROM A SUPER BORING PARTY!
THERE'S ONLY ONE THING THAT CAN GET ME OUT OF THIS...
WHAT...THE HELL?!
WOF!
NICE KIDDO?!

...ALCOHOL.
CLIN
FIRED!
YOU SHOULD HAVE SEEN HIM CRYING OVER HIS MORTGAGE!
MUAHAHAHAHA!
HI HI! PLEASE, TELL ME HE FELL TO HIS KNEES! THEY ALWAYS DO THAT!
ONE TIME, A GUY EVEN BROUGHT OUT PHOTOS OF HIS KIDS!
HI HI!
HI HI!
HA HA!
HA HA!
YEAH, AND WHAT ABOUT THAT TIME THE PRINT SHOP RAN OUR BOOK COVERS UPSIDE DOWN?!
WE TOOK THEM TO COURT SO HARD, THE ONLY THING THE GUY PRINTS THESE DAYS IS HIS AUNT'S PIZZA MENUS!
UNBELIEVABLE, I'VE BEEN TALKING AND LAUGHING FOR A HALF HOUR!
I STILL WANT TO GO HOME...BUT I'M HAVING FUN! AND SO IS ZA'ATAR!
WOW! STILL GOING ON ABOUT BOREDOM, ANISETTE?
NOT THAT THIS IS ABOUT HER...
OR ABOUT SHOWING BURNET I KNOW HOW TO HAVE FUN.
NO SIR!
I'VE GOT NOTHING TO PROVE! I'M JUST ENJOYING A NICE CONVERSATION WITHOUT FEELING THE PRESSURE AT ALL!
THIS IS NOT A COMPETITION!
STILL, I SHOULDN'T EXAGGERATE...
ALL THIS DRINKING'S WARMING ME UP, OR MAYBE...
I'D LOVE TO HEAR MORE OF YOUR STORIES, BUT I'VE GOT AN EARLY FLIGHT, TOMORROW...
ALREADY?

YES, SADLY. ♥
UH?
THESE THINGS ARE USUALLY A BORE, I STRUGGLE TO FAKE MY INTEREST...
BUT YOU'VE BEEN AMAZING COMPANY. THANKS TO YOU, THIS NIGHT WAS ACTUALLY ENJOYABLE.
YEAH...
I DO HOPE WE CAN STAY IN TOUCH.
...THAT'S NOT THE ALCOHOL...
I MEAN...
NOT JUST AS FAR AS WORK GOES.
IF THAT'S SOMETHING YOU'D LIKE.
I FEEL LIKE BOTH OF US...
...HAVE A LOT IN COMMON... ♥
DON'T PANIC!
DO NOT SCREW THIS UP!
DO NOT FUCK THIS UP! DON'T...

WHY SHOULD WE RUIN THIS NIGHT WITH SUCH A QUICK GOODBYE...
...WHEN WE COULD HEAD TO THE BATHROOM AND TRULY SEE EACH OTHER OFF?
SUCH...SUCH BOLDNESS! ♥
I KNOW, I... I'M ALWAYS HEARING THAT. ♥
YOU KNOW, MAYBE IT'S THE ALCOHOL TALKING... BUT WHO CARES?
STRUSSH
I CERTAINLY DON'T!
SBAM

I DESERVE THIS!
I THOUGHT YOU WERE TOO MUCH OF A SNOB FOR A QUICKIE ON THE TOILET...
THIS IS A BIG STEP UP FROM MISSIONARY WITH SOCKS ON, LIKE LAST TIME!
ANYTHING ELSE I CAN DO FOR YOU, MISS PAPRIKA?
ANF!
ANF!
ANF!
ANF!
ANF!
SAY SOMETHING SEXY, AND GO FASTERRRR...
THAAAANKSSSS
OHHH, YEAH, GO OOOONNNH
ANF!
ANF!
YOUR SALARY'S ABOUT TO INCREASE BY 50%...
...AND SO WILL YOUR LIBIDO!
ANF!
WE'LL LIVE IN AN ENORMOUS MANSION AT VESUVIUS. ANISETTE WILL DIE OF JEALOUSY, BUT ONLY AFTER LOSING HER HAIR!
ANF!
ANF!
DON'T S-STOOOOAHHHHGGG
AGAIN WITH THESE DISGUSTING THOUGHTS?

YOU JUST CAN'T STOP WHORING EFT AND IGHT INSIDE OUR HEAD!
LYING DOWN FOR RANDOM PEOPLE!
THIS ONE YOU ONLY MET A HALF HOUR AGO!
YOUR WHOLE LIFE IS WORK AND IMAGINARY SEX. PATHETIC!
DAD?! CAN'T YOU JUST LET ME CUM IN PEACE?!
MAYBE HE'S THE ONE! AND ALSO... YOU'RE A WORKAHOLIC TOO!
ANF!
ANF!
IT'S DIFFERENT, I'M A MAN!
AND NOBODY CARES ABOUT YOUR OPINION!
ANF!
ZA-ZA'ATAR WOULD CARE! I THINK...
PFFT! HE'S NO DIFFERENT THAN ME!
WILL YOU SHUT UP AND LET ME FINISH, PAPPY!?
OH, YES, ES, YOU'RE IGHT, RIGHT, IIIIGGHHHHT...!
ANF!
NF!
ANF!
AHHHH!
ANF!

FRUSH
...
...I THINK IT MIGHT BE GOOD TO STAY IN TOUCH...ON WORK TERMS, THAT IS...FOR SPICE IT UP!
OH, OF COURSE! EHM...
SORRY, I DIDN'T MEAN TO EMBARRASS YOU!
SO...SEE YOU SOON?
YE-YES, SOON...
CONGRATS, PAPRIKA! THIS IS YOUR BILLIONTH SELF-SABOTAGE BY INCLUDING YOUR NAGGING DAD IN YOUR PORN FANTASY.
ARGH... THAT SENTENCE SOUNDS SO WRONG!
I'LL BE RIGHT BACK.
"OF COURSE I'D LIKE TO KEEP IN TOUCH, ZA'ATAR!" WAS THAT SO HARD TO SAY?
SCREW ME, AND SCREW MY STUPID BRAIN!
MAYBE WITH A FEW MORE DRINKS, YEAH...
MAYBE THEN I COULD GET MYSELF TOGETHER... GO FIND HIM, MAYBE HE'S STILL HERE...
ZA'ATAR JUST LEFT... ARE YOU OKAY?
I SAW WHAT HAPPENED.
...OF COURSE!

ACTUALLY, YOU DO.
LET ME HANDLE THIS, PAPPY.
!
IF YOU WANT TO HIT ON ZA'ATAR, GO AHEAD. BUT LET ME GIVE YOU A COUPLE OF TIPS... AS YOUR FRIEND.
I-I WASN'T HITTING ON HIM. HE WAS THE ONE...
I KNOW YOU, YOU SILLY GIRL.
YOU TOOK HIS POLITENESS AS SOMETHING MORE. YOU STARTED BEING FLIRTY...
...THINKING THE DRINKS WOULD SOMEHOW MAKE YOU CHARMING.
YOU'RE DRUNK...AND UNBUTTONED. WHAT WERE YOU EVEN TRYING TO DO, UNDRESS?
BUT YOU SHOULD KNOW...ZA'ATAR IS SERIOUS. WAY MORE THAN I AM. I'M NOT SURE HE COULD BE INTERESTED IN A GIRL LIKE...GOD, HOW CAN I SAY THIS NICELY? LET'S JUST SAY...
A GIRL LIKE YOU!
THERE YOU GO!
NOW YOU SEEM LIKE A GOOD GIRL!
I'M SO STUPID.

I'LL NEVER BE ABLE TO TALK TO ZA'ATAR, LIKE EVER AGAIN...NOT AFTER LEAVING HIM AT THE BAR LIKE THAT.
I WISH I COULD JUST SAY, "SCREW THIS, I DON'T NEED HIM! I'M A DRAGON"... BECAUSE I'M A STRONG WOMAN AND ALL THAT STUFF... BUT I CAN'T.
I WISH I WAS, I MEAN THAT!
34
I'M JUST A BORING GIRL WHO WANTS SOMEONE AT HER SIDE, SOMEONE WHO CARES ABOUT HER, BESIDES HER FAMILY. I JUST WANT TO FEEL WELCOMED, AND HAVE FRIENDSHIPS OUTSIDE OF WORK.
HELL
HOW DOES EVERYONE MAKE IT LOOK SO EASY? MAYBE IT IS EASY, AND I'M JUST TRULY THAT WEIRD.
MY HEAD'S SPINNING, I DON'T KNOW WHERE I'M GOING...HELL, ADMITTING THAT IS SO HUMILIATING...
AND I'M STILL AROUSED BY THAT STUPID SCENARIO. THAT'S THE TRUTH! I'M SOME KIND OF FRUSTRATED PERVERT!
WITH NO FRIENDS, WITH NO ONE!
PATHETIC!
AND SINCE I'M PATHETIC, LONELY AND DRUNK, JUST THIS ONE TIME...
MISS PAPRIKA?
WHAT'S GOING ON?
...I WANT TO HIT BOTTOM, AND SLEEP WITH THE FIRST DUDE I FIND.
IS EVERYTH OKAY?

WOW! YOUR HOUSE IS AMAZING!
YOU'RE SUCH AN IDIOT! THIS IS YOUR HOUSE! MUAHAHAHA!
THEY WERE YOUR KEYS, DON'T YOU REMEMBER?!
EHM... YOU GAVE ME THEM BECAUSE YOU KEPT MISSING THE KEYHOLE!
AH, RIGHT...
BESIDES, MY HOUSE IS A CLOSET COMPARED TO THIS.
YEAH, A DELIVERY BOY LIKE YOU WOULD SLEEP IN A SHITHOLE.
SPEAKING OF SLEEPING, AND HITTING THE KEYHOLE...
YOU STILL NEED TO SEE MY GORGEOUS BEDROOM! ♥
THAT'S WHY WE'RE HERE, RIGHT?
HE HE HE! ♥
WOW, THAT'S KING-SIZE, FOR SURE!
WHAT A COINCIDENCE...
...I'M HOPING TO SAY THE SAME ABOUT YOU! NOW TAKE OFF YOUR PANTS!
WOOF!
ZA'ATAR... ♥
I'M SORRY ABOUT THIS... SNIFF
LET'S SEE TO YOUR NEEDS, YEAH?

BOING
EXACTLY! LADIES FIRST!
AT WORK, EVERYONE TALKS ABOUT YOUR...YOUR CANNEDLAMBO... YOUR CUNNINGLINGO... YOUR WHATEVER IT'S CALLED...AND HOW GREAT YOU ARE AT IT!
MY EX WOULDN'T EVEN TRY, SO GET TO WORK! I'VE GOT HIGH EXPECTATIONS!
BIG HALO ENERG
EHY♥
MUAHAHAHA!
WHAT'S WRONG? THAT PLUSHIE OF YOURS GOT YOUR TONGUE?
I HOPE NOT...YOU'RE GOING TO NEED IT!
AHR AHR-AHR!
BURP
TREAT ME NICELY, AND I'LL RECIPROCATE...

YEAH, SO... LET'S JUST COVER THIS, OKAY?!
?
GOSH! THIS BLANKET, WITH THE LITTLE PEPPERS... THAT'S SO CUTE!
PAT PAT
YOU'RE REJECTING ME? YOU? YOUUU?!
THE WEIRDO THAT CALLS HIMSELF DILL-DO, THAT KEEPS HIS GLASSES ON AT NIGHT?!
THE BIG MAN THAT WALKS AROUND WITH THE SMALLEST DOG POSSIBLE IN HIS PURSE?!
WOOF!
GRR
I DON'T KNOW, MAYBE I'M A BIT WEIRD...
DADDY PREFERS THE TERM "SPECIAL."
BUT I'D BE OUT OF MY MIND TO SLEEP WITH SOMEONE SO DRUNK THEY DON'T RECOGNIZE THEIR OWN HOME.
NOT TO MENTION, YOUR FACE!
ARE YOU CALLING ME UGLY?!
NO! THAT'S NOT WHAT I MEAN!
YOU'RE LIKE... A MASCARA FOUNTAIN!
WHAT HAPPENED TO YOU? WHO IS THIS... "ZATARIO"?

UGHHH
SNIFF!
SNIFF!
IF I BEHAVE? I DON'T GET WHAT I WANT. IF I DON'T BEHAVE? I STILL DON'T GET IT!
SOMEONE LIKE YOU COULD NEVER UNDERSTAND HOW I FEEL!
SNIFF!
SNIFF!
SOMEONE LIKE ME?!
YOU KNOW EXACTLY WHAT I MEAN!
YOU'VE GOT THE FACE, THE HALO, THE BODY AND THE PERFECT JERK SMILE...EVEN IF YOU'RE LAZY, AND SPEND MOST OF THE DAY IN FRONT OF THE MIRROR FLEXING, YOU CAN DO AND SAY WHATEVER YOU WANT!
YOU FANCY A GIRL? YOU FUCK HER!
YOU WANT FRIENDS? EVERYBODY ADORES YOU!
EVEN IF YOU ARE DUMB AS A BOWL OF SOUP.
AND THEN THERE'S ME. I HAVE TO FIGHT EVERY DAY FOR PEOPLE'S FEAR AND RESPECT. EVERYONE HATES ME, AND I CAN'T EVEN GET FUCKED BY AN IDIOT LIKE YOU!
YOU MUST'VE HAD AN ALL-TIME BAD DAY, I WON'T BOTHER YOU ANYMORE. BUT I JUST WANT TO SAY...YOU'RE NOT AS BAD AS YOU THINK, AND MAYBE...I'M NOT THAT BAD EITHER, OKAY?
SO WHEN YOU SOBER UP, IF YOU STILL FEEL THIS LONELY, WELL...GIVE ME A CALL! IF EVERYONE DOES ADORE ME LIKE YOU SAY...MAYBE THERE'S A REASON FOR THAT.
SLEEP TIGHT!
SNIFF...
CLICK
SNIFF...
SNIFFZZZZZ!

I CAN'T SLEEP.
I PUKED, I SHOWERED... MAYBE I'LL OPEN SOME OF YESTERDAY'S PACKAGES.
05:45 am
NEWS
ANYTHING TO STOP MY MIND FROM THINKING ABOUT IT, OVER AND OVER AGAIN...
ALWAYS ABOUT LAST NIGHT...AND DILL.
I REMEMBER JUST ENOUGH TO KNOW HOW BADLY I TREATED HIM...AND HOW I EMBARRASSED MYSELF IN FRONT OF ZA'ATAR...
WHAT WOULD DAD THINK IF HE KNEW ABOUT YESTERDAY?!
FIRST, MOM LEAVES HIM FOR SOMEONE ELSE, THEN HIS HEART ATTACK, AND NOW...A DAUGHTER LIKE ME.
WHAT RIGHT DO I HAVE TO COMPLAIN?
CRAVING THE SEX I DON'T HAVE JUST MAKES ME SAD. CRAVING THE FRIENDS I DON'T HAVE MAKES ME SADDER. I JUST NEED TO STOP, IT'S SO OBVIOUS.
STOP THINKING ABOUT THOSE THINGS, STOP CRAVING THOSE THINGS.
DAD NEVER GOT MARRIED AGAIN, AND THE FEW FRIENDS HE DOES HAVE ARE FROM WORK. AND LOOK AT HIM!
HE'S GOT A HUMBLE, RESPECTABLE LIFE!
HE HAS IT GOOD!
...SICKNESS ASIDE.
YEAH, SO...A LIFE LIKE THE ONE I ALREADY HAVE...BUT MINUS THE COMPLICATIONS. THAT SHOULD BE EASY!
WHAT?
THAT'S THE MYSTERIOUS BOX FROM YESTERDAY!
A USB DRIVE?
128GB
IF IT'S FROM SOME SECRET ADMIRER WELL...THEN THAT'S THE MOST USELESS GIFT EVER. WHO EVEN STILL USES THESE?
READ ME LATER...
MAYBE IT'S SOME KIND OF MESSAGE...
IF IT'S CREEPY SOMEHOW...

HERE, LET'S TAKE A LOOK...
PLAY
?
A VIDEO?! WHAT THE HELL?!
YOUR HONOR!
WHAT'S HAPPENING?
NNNGHHHH
IS THIS COCAINE NOT TO YOUR LIKING, SIR?
ARTE-ARTEMISIO...?!
SIR?!
MOVE, YOU IDIOTS! CAN'T YOU SEE GRANDPA HERE IS HAVING A HEART ATTACK?!
SOMEONE CALL AN AMBULANCE!
BUT DON'T TELL A SOUL, YOU HEAR ME? NO ONE CAN KNOW ABOUT THIS!
NOT A SINGLE PERS--
BZZZZZZ

CHAPTER 4

I THINK I KNOW WHO I WANT TO BE!

AND SO... WHEN THE COUSIN OF THE BROTHER OF MY COUSIN'S HUSBAND SHOWED ME THE GUEST LIST FROM THAT SEX-FEST AT HIS PLACE, I JUST COULDN'T RESIST.
A SIMPLE HIDDEN CAMERA WOULD SUFFICE.
IT WAS MY CHANCE, AFTER ALL.
I COULD FINALLY GET BACK AT YOU AND...
SORRY, DID I SOMEHOW GIVE THE IMPRESSION I WANTED A CONVERSATION?
TAKE THE MONEY AND FUCK OFF.
WHAT?!
AREN'T YOU CURIOUS ABOUT WHO I-
=COUGH=
COFF COFF
PLEASE...
IT'D TAKE MORE THAN SMOKE TO COVER UP THAT COLOGNE.
I COULD SPOT YOU A MILE AWAY.
AH, WELL... THEN YOU CAN PROBABLY GUESS MY MOTIVATIONS.
SO, IF YOU DON'T WANT YOUR BIG-TIME JUDGE OF A FATHER TO BE ROCKED BY A SCANDAL...
THE GREAT, UNDERPAID CHAM IS DUE A HEFTY SEVERANCE.

COME TO THINK OF IT, YOUR REPUTATION WOULD BE COMPROMISED TOO.
MAYBE I SHOULD SELL THIS TO THE PRESS.
IT WOULD BE SO SATISFY--
...UH?!
WOOSH
SBAM
YOU SEE, CHAM...
I KNOW I CAN BE A REALLY DEMANDING BOSS.
FOR A MOMENT THERE, I EVEN THOUGHT THAT MAYBE I CROSS THE LINE SOMETIMES.
BUT ONLY FOR A MOMENT.
OUCH!
AHI AHI!
CRACK
I THOUGHT MAYBE I COULD STAND TO BE A BIT MORE COMPASSIONATE TO POOR LITTLE FRESHLY GRADUATED CHAM...
BUT THEN AGAIN...

LIFE IS ABOUT CHANGE.
COLLEGE, JOBS... WE'RE ALWAYS ON THE MOVE.
AND NOW, IT'S TIME FOR YOU TO DO SOME CHANGING.
FROM A POST-GRADUATE NOBODY TO A JOB-SEEKING NOBODY.
AND BELIEVE ME WHEN I TELL YOU... THE LIST OF PEOPLE IN THIS CITY WHO OWE ME OR MY DAD IS LONG.
SO, IF I WERE YOU, I'D THINK TWICE ABOUT SPREADING THAT VIDEO.
IF A SINGLE FRAME OF THAT GETS OUT, THE STENCH OF THE HOT DOG CART YOU'LL END UP WORKING WILL BE THE ONLY THING COMPETING WITH YOUR DISGUSTING COLOGNE.

I CAN'T WAIT FOR CASTING TO START! ♥
UH... YEAH, YEAH, BURNET.
WHY THE LONG FACE, ZA'ATAR? SECOND THOUGHTS ABOUT SETTLING FOR BUSINESS CLASS?
LOOK, THEY'VE STILL GOT CHAMPAGNE. THAT'S A SMALL TRACE OF CIVILIZATION.
MH.
PLEASE, TELL ME ALL THESE "MH"'S ARE ABOUT THIS AND NOT MISS PAPPY.
WELL, I HAVEN'T GIVEN UP YET...
...BUT NO, THIS ISN'T ABOUT HER.
OTHER STUFF ON MY MIND.
AS YOUR FRIEND, AND AS HER EX, LET ME TELL YOU: WHAT HAPPENED WAS FOR THE BEST.
YOU DIDN'T MISS A THING!
ALL THAT SAID...IT WILL BE NICE TO SEE HER AGAIN.
THERE'RE NO DOUBT COUNTLESS BUSINESS LUNCHES AHEAD WHERE WE COULD GET TO KNOW EACH OTHER.
AND THEN, MAYBE...
MH... ♥

GOOD MOOORNING, LADIES! ♥
INFERNUM PRESS
WEIRD. I DON'T HEAR MISS PAPRIKA YELLING, SHE SEEMS TOO QUIET...
MAYBE I SHOULD CHECK ON HER AFTER LAST NIGHT...
OH, THERE SHE IS! HEY! ♥
!
EVERYTHING OKAY?
SO-SORRY MOM, WHAT WERE YOU SAYING?!
DAD'S STILL ON THE PLANE?
I GET IT...
NO, NOTHING, IT'S FINE...
...
I...JUST WANTED TO TELL HIM SOMETHING.
DON'T WORRY! I SAID EVERYTHING'S FI-FINE!
TOTALLY FINE! BYE!

HONEY, ARE YOU SURE THAT-- BIP.
- NEWS -
The judge's condition after his heart attack seems to have stabilized.
It appears he'll be headed to Italy to take some time off.
"I can't wait to get back in court" said Artemisio.
-COVERS -DEEP BEYOND VOL. 1 -FIRE F. ANECIA
EVERYTHING'S FINE, THAT'S FOR SURE.
I'VE GOT SO MUCH TO WORK ON RIGHT NOW...BUT I CAN'T GET THIS OUT OF MY HEAD.
I JUST WANT TO SPEAK WITH HIM... JUST WANT AN EXPLANATION. I WANT TO KNOW WHO MY FATHER REALLY IS. HE CAN'T BE THE SAME PERSON FROM THAT DISGUSTING VIDEO.
HE CAN'T BE THE KIND OF DEPRAVED DEVIL HE ALWAYS ORDERED ME NOT TO BE! NOT HIM!
IT DOESN'T MAKE ANY SENSE!
MISS... PAPRIKA?
I'M SORRY... IT'S ALMOST LUNCHTIME, AND WE STILL NEED THE COVER APPROVALS, PLUS THE CONTRACTS TO FIX AND...
IS EVERYTHING OKAY?
LUNCH, EH? USUALLY IT'S CHAM GETTING ME LUNCH, BUT I...
...I COMPLETELY FORGOT.
BETTER SKIP IT.
I'LL NEED THAT TIME TO CATCH UP ON WORK.
...

...WITH SOUTH AFRICAN GINGER, AND A COUPLE OF DROPS OF EXTRA-AGED, THIRD-GENERATION PORTUGUESE OLIVE OIL.
EHM... WE DON'T HAVE THOSE INGREDIENTS, I'VE ALREADY TOLD YOU. MULTIPLE TIMES.
THIS IS JUST A REGULAR SALAD.
PLEASE, TELL ME IT'S AT LEAST LOCALLY SOURCED.
YES, MISS. OUR GARDEN IS JUST PAST THE CROSSROAD LIGHTS ON SEVENTH.
I GUESS HUMOR GETS YOU FARTHER THAN A DEGREE AROUND HERE.
C-COULD YOU BRING US SOME ICE?
PLEASE!
LOVE...YOU PROMISED ME A LUNCH ALONE, JUST THE TWO OF US. AND PIZZA. YOU PROMISED ME PIZZA. YOU'RE ALMOST NEVER HOME, AND...
I KNOW, NORI! BUT WHAT WAS I SUPPOSED TO DO?
SHE SEEMED SO DOWN. I COULDN'T STAND TO LEAVE HER SO DEPRESSED.
ICE CREAM
YOU KNOW I CAN HEAR YOU, RIGHT?
I'M USED TO THE GOSSIP OF DISOBEDIENT SUBORDINATES, I'VE GOT YEARS OF EXPERIENCE THERE.
JUST LET ME FINISH THIS NIGHTMARE THEY CALL A SALAD AND I'LL GLADLY LEAVE YOU ALONE.

WAIT, MISS!
MY WIFE AND I ARE JUST WORRIED ABOUT YOU!
WHEN ASSESSING A NEW NOVEL, I ALWAYS CHECK FOR INTERESTING LEADS.
NOT PERFECT, THAT IS. NOT AT ALL. IT'S LOSERS AMONG OTHER LOSERS THAT ARE THE DRAW.
WITHOUT THEM AND THEIR WILD WAYS, SOMETIMES THE PROTAGONIST WOULDN'T HAVE ANYTHING TO DO.
ALL MY LIFE, MY FATH--EHRM, SOMEONE I VALUE ALWAYS TOLD ME TO BEHAVE IN A CERTAIN WAY. AND...I DID.
IF I'M THE PROTAGONIST OF THIS STORY...AND THESE LICKERS ARE THE MOST SIMILAR THING I HAVE TO SIDEKICKS... I MAY TRY...
BUT I BEHAVED SO WELL THAT I'M AFRAID TO STOP, EVEN IF BEHAVING MAKES ME MISERABLE...
AND, IRONICALLY... THIS PERSON WAS NOT WHO HE SAID HE WAS. NOW, I THINK HE MAYBE BUILT HIS ENTIRE EXISTENCE ON LIES...THAT I FELL FOR.
WAS I RIGHT TO WASTE ALL THESE YEARS BEING PARANOID ABOUT SITUATIONS OTHERS WOULD FIND PERFECTLY NORMAL?
I'M NOT SURE I UNDERSTAND, BUT... MAYBE IT'S TIME TO BE MORE HONEST WITH YOURSELF AND REALLY THINK ABOUT WHO YOU WANT TO BE. THAT, AND WHAT YOU REALLY DESIRE.
IF YOU TRY TO LIVE UP TO EVERYONE ELSE'S EXPECTATIONS, YOU'LL NEVER FIND TIME FOR YOURSELF.

BUT... I'M NOT SURE WHAT I WANT...
BESIDES A BETTER LUNCH, THAT IS...
JUST LOOK AROUND.
FIND OUT WHO YOU WANT TO BE, AND BECOME HER!
UNDERSTAND WHAT YOU WANT AND GO GET IT!
IT'S EASY!
WHO DO I WANT TO BE? WHAT DO I WANT? EH...
VERSACELA. DEVILINO. LOUIS DIAVOLON. ALL THOSE GUYS! ♥
THE GREAT ANTIDEPRESSANT OF THE SUCCESSFUL, EDUCATED WOMEN OF THE WORLD, THAT'S WHAT I WANT!
VERSACELA
D&A
DIAVOLINO
EMPORIO ARMAROS
ANGELRRY LONDON
BEING RICH AND HAVING SO MANY OUTFITS THAT I NEVER WEAR THE SAME ONE TWICE. ♥
BUT...
I'VE DONE IT, EVERY FRIDAY AFTER WORK.
I'M REALLY HAPPY, BUT IT'S NOT ENOUGH.
MAYBE NORI IS RIGHT, I HAVE TO LOOK AROUND...
I NEED A SIGN.
♪ QUESTA È UNA STATION WAGON... ♫

DAD?! YOU OLD BASTARD!
HOW LONG DO YOU EXPECT ME TO WAIT--
UH... MI-MISS PAPRIKA?
THAT VOICE... ZA'ATAR?
IS--IS IT A BAD TIME? I KNOW IT'S LATE...
MI-MISTER... ZA...ZA'AT...
I'M SORRY TO BARGE IN. I WANTED TO APOLOGIZE FOR LAST NIGHT. I'VE BEEN...LESS THAN PROFESSIONAL.
WHAT?!
NOT AT ALL!
OH, WELL... THANKS! I'M GLAD TO HEAR THAT!
I'VE JUST BEEN EXHAUSTED, THESE PAST FEW DAYS HAVE BEEN HELL. AND SPICE IT UP! IS EATING UP ALL MY TIME...
I GET IT. WE'RE UNDER A TON OF PRESSURE HERE AS WELL, ME MOST OF ALL. AND ABOUT THAT, I WAS CONSIDERING SOMETHING... IF YOU AGREE.
OH, SURE. PLEASE, GO ON!
IN A FEW WEEKS, THERE'LL BE AN IMPORTANT INTERNATIONAL MARKET IN ITALY.
YES, I GO EVERY YEAR WITH OUR PRODUCT DEPARTMENT.
USUALLY, I TAKE THE CHANCE TO VISIT MY RELATIVES...
THAT'S GREAT. I'LL BE THERE!
NOT TO SEE YOUR FAMILY, OF COURSE! I MEAN...
THAT IS...UNLESS YOU WANT ME TO.
FOR REAL?

RIGHT NOW, WE BOTH HAVE TOO MUCH ON OUR PLATES.
AND WE'RE ALSO SO FAR AWAY FROM EACH OTHER. IN ITALY, IT'LL BE DIFFERENT...
WE COULD PICK UP WHERE WE LEFT OFF LAST TIME.
WOW, THAT ONE IS NICE!
OR, IF YOU WANT...
...WE COULD START ALL OVER AGAIN.
MY DAD WOULD DIE IF HE SAW ME IN A DRESS LIKE THAT!
HA HA!
EMPORIO ARMAROS
WE COULD GET TO KNOW EACH OTHER SO MUCH BETTER...
NO MATTER HOW MUCH WORK TRIES TO GET IN THE WAY.
MAYBE I GOT IT.
I THINK I KNOW WHO I WANT TO BE...
UNTIL THEN, LET'S KEEP OUR RELATIONSHIP STRICTLY PROFESSIONAL, SO WE CAN BRING THIS JOB HOME.
I MEAN, THAT'S IF YOU LIKE THE IDEA AT ALL, OF COURSE...
I THINK IT'S A SPLENDID IDEA.
...AND WHO I WANT TO HAVE.

I DON'T KNOW...I'VE NEVER WORN SOMETHING LIKE THIS BEFORE.
TRUST ME, YOU LOOK TOTALLY DEVILISH!
DO YOU LIKE IT?
YES!
MAYBE HE'LL LIKE IT AS WELL.
I'M JUST GOING TO TRY A FEW MORE THINGS... MEET ME AT THE COUNTER?
I'M SO NERVOUS.
HOW SILLY IS THAT?
IT'S ONLY A DRESS. A DRESS WITH...
...A VERY LOW CUT.

YOU'RE BACK AT IT!
THIS TIME WE WON'T STOP... RIGHT, MISS PAPRIKA?
ARE YOU CRAZY? IN PUBLIC? YOU'RE BREAKING AT LEAST TEN LOCAL LAWS!
YEAH, AGAINST BEING A DIRTY SLU--
FUCK OFF!
FLA
ASH
NICE! THAT'S HOW I LIKE YOU...
NO FUCKS GIVEN ABOUT ANYTHING OR ANYONE...
...AND ALWAYS STRAIGHT TO THE POINT!

OUFFF...
AH, SWEET BEELZEBUB!
I CAN'T BELIEVE IT! I GOT AWAY WITH IT!
WHO'S GOT A SMOKE?
HE HE HE...
!
?
...
IS... THAT A SMILE?

MAYBE I TOOK THINGS A BIT TOO FAST...
BUT YOU KNOW WHAT? FUCK IT. I'LL DO WHAT I WANT!
PLUS... I NEED THE PRACTICE.
WHAT LITTLE SEX I HAVE HAD HAS BEEN...BAD. AND A LONG TIME AGO.
I CAN'T LET ZA'ATAR DOWN WHEN THE TIME COMES.
HELL, YOU'RE INSATIABLE! PLUS, THOSE GLASSES? YOU'VE GOT ME GOING! ♥
DEH HE HE!
OLÈ! ♥
ABOUT THAT...TIME TO LET MY IMAGINATION RUN WILD.
YOU-- YOU DO THIS OFTEN?
ERM, ALL...ALL THE TIME!
"OLÈ"...?
LISTEN, COULD... YOU CALL ME MISS PAPRIKA?
HA HA HA!
HELL YES, MISS PAPRIKA!
I'M HERE TO GRANT YOUR EVERY WISH... ♥
ZIIIP
MY WISHES, HUH? SEEMS NICE ENOUGH. ♥
MAYBE I WAS RIGHT AFTER ALL--

JUST OPEN YOUR LITTLE MOUTH... ♥
UH?!
IMPRESSED, EH? I GET IT.
EVERY MORNING I GET UP, AND IT'S HARD TO STOP STARING AT IT...
YOU SHOULD HEAR THE EXCUSES I HAVE TO MAKE UP FOR MY BOSS!
I-I DON'T UNDERSTAND.
I WANTED TO GO WILD, BUT... I'M PETRIFIED. NOT EXCITED AT ALL.
NOT TO MENTION THIS GUY IS RUDE...
HE'S NOT DOING ANYTHING TO MAKE ME COMFORTABLE. HE'S JUST INTERESTED IN HIS JUNK.
WHAT'S WRONG?! I'M SWEATING A LITTLE, BUT I JUST SHOWERED. I SWEAR!
COME ON, WE'RE WASTING TIME... ♥
GET THE FUCK OFF ME!
IS THIS HOW IT'S ALWAYS GOING TO BE?

OH YES, IT IS...AND WORSE.
COME ON, JUST FORGET ALL THIS WHORING.
GET OUT OF MY HEAD!
WHAT IF IT HADN'T BEEN IN A SHOP?
WHAT IF HE WAS MAD ON TOP OF BEING RUDE?
NOTHING HAPPENED.
BUT IT COULD'VE. AND YOU WOULD'VE DESERVED IT!
LIKE EVERY SLUT OUT THERE LOOKING FOR TROUBLE.
YOUR KIND NEEDS CORRECTING. JUST LIKE BURNET DID...
OKAY, WOW! YOU CAN DEFINITELY FUCK OFF, NOW.
AT LEAST FOR A FEW MINUTES, OKAY?
I FROZE UP WITH THAT GUY, BUT HE WAS AN IDIOT. WHAT HAPPENS IF I FREEZE WITH ZA'ATAR?
I CAN'T LET HIM KNOW HOW FUCKED UP I AM. I WANT A NORMAL RELATIONSHIP, PLEASANT ALL AROUND, LIKE OTHER PEOPLE HAVE.
I NEED TO BEHAVE LIKE I'M AT WORK: PERFECT, AND UP TO EVERYONE'S EXPECTATIONS...
BOTH MINE...AND WHICHEVER DEVIL I'M INTERESTED IN.
IF I'M GOING TO PRACTICE ON AN IDIOT, MIGHT AS WELL BE SOMEONE MORE DOCILE.

YOU OKAY, DILL?
!
YOU HAVEN'T TOUCHED YOUR DINNER, KID...
AND I EVEN COOKED YOUR FAVORITE... MASHED PIZZA!
IT'S MISS PAPRIKA. SHE TEXTED ME...
...AND WANTS ME TO SPEND THE NIGHT.
THE ONE THAT ALWAYS TALKS DOWN TO YOU?
THAT DIDN'T EVEN SAY HELLO TO YOU TODAY? THAT ONE?
THAT NEVER EVEN THANKS YOU FOR A DAMN THING?
YOU KNOW WHAT I THINK?
SCREW HER!
BUT NOT LITERALLY.
YOU'RE NOT HER PET.
MH...
PIZZA!
YOU WANT TO BE THE OFFICE SEX TOY AT INFERNUM PRESS? FINE. GO AHEAD. BUT SET SOME BOUNDARIES, KID.
TRY TO HOLD ON TO A BIT OF YOUR DIGNITY.
BAM
RIGHT. THANKS. I'M OUT.
...FANTASTIC.

DO YOU KNOW HOW LONG I'VE WAITED FOR THIS?
KEEP IT COOL, DUDE.
OR YOU WON'T MAKE IT PAST THE DOOR.
AFTER ALL THESE YEARS IGNORING ME...YOU DON'T GET IT.
YOU WERE THE ONLY ONE MISSING. I'M SO HAPPY... I'M FUCKING HONORED. ♥
WOULD YOU JUST SHUT UP AND LOOK AT THE BOX, YOU STUPID PENGUIN?!
BOING
WHY DO I CARE WHAT'S IN SOME STUPID BOX?
IT'S A PROJECTOR, YOU MORON.
GIVE ME A SECOND.
TRY TO DIRECT SOME BLOOD FROM YOUR GENITALS TO THE TWO NEURONS YOU HAVE LEFT, OKAY?
FIVE MINUTES SHOULD DO IT.
OH.

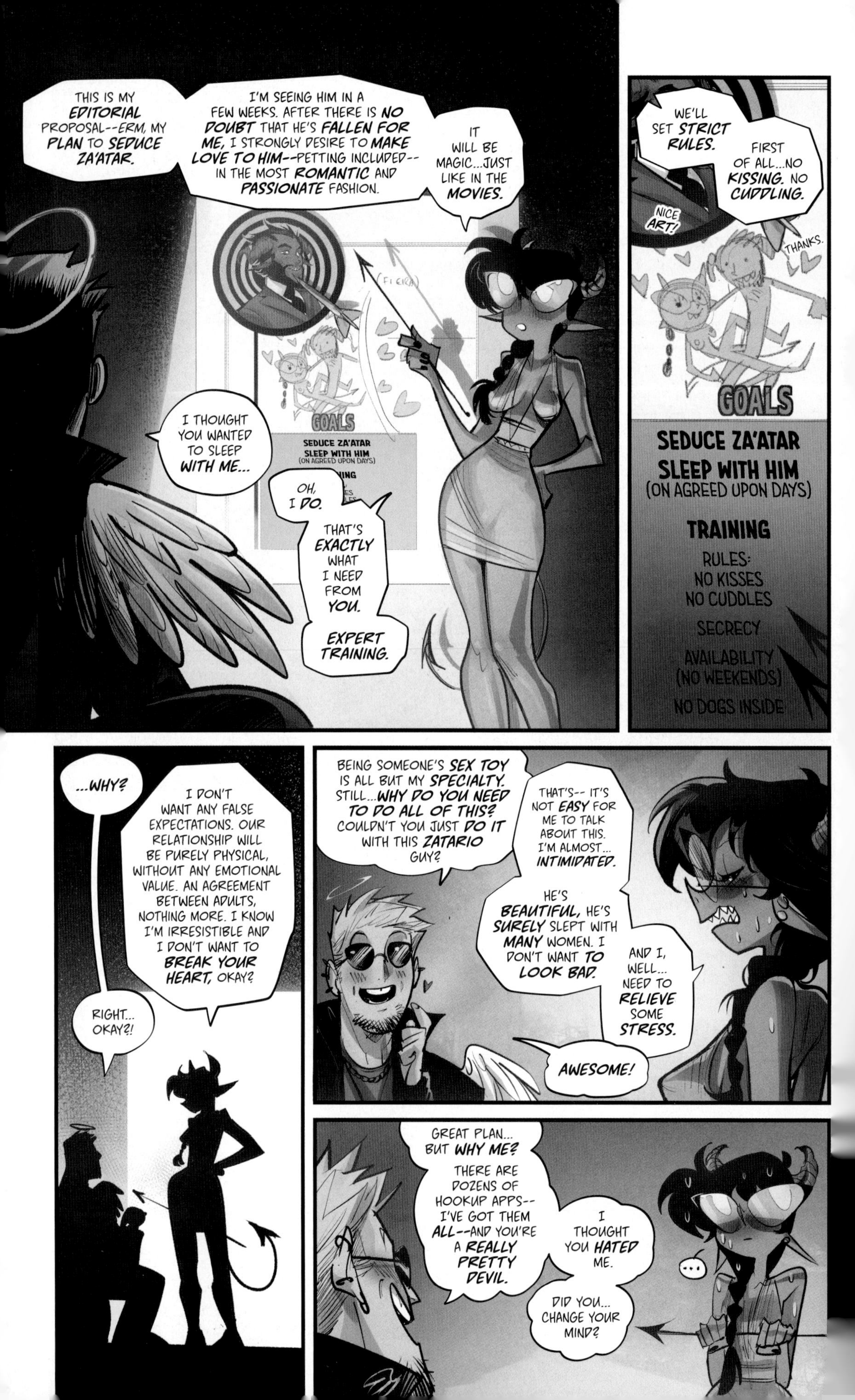

THIS IS MY EDITORIAL PROPOSAL--ERM, MY PLAN TO SEDUCE ZA'ATAR.
I'M SEEING HIM IN A FEW WEEKS. AFTER THERE IS NO DOUBT THAT HE'S FALLEN FOR ME, I STRONGLY DESIRE TO MAKE LOVE TO HIM--PETTING INCLUDED--IN THE MOST ROMANTIC AND PASSIONATE FASHION.
IT WILL BE MAGIC...JUST LIKE IN THE MOVIES.
I THOUGHT YOU WANTED TO SLEEP WITH ME...
OH, I DO.
THAT'S EXACTLY WHAT I NEED FROM YOU.
EXPERT TRAINING.
WE'LL SET STRICT RULES.
FIRST OF ALL...NO KISSING. NO CUDDLING.
NICE ART!
THANKS.
GOALS
SEDUCE ZA'ATAR
SLEEP WITH HIM
(ON AGREED UPON DAYS)
TRAINING
RULES:
NO KISSES
NO CUDDLES
SECRECY
AVAILABILITY
(NO WEEKENDS)
NO DOGS INSIDE
...WHY?
I DON'T WANT ANY FALSE EXPECTATIONS. OUR RELATIONSHIP WILL BE PURELY PHYSICAL, WITHOUT ANY EMOTIONAL VALUE. AN AGREEMENT BETWEEN ADULTS, NOTHING MORE. I KNOW I'M IRRESISTIBLE AND I DON'T WANT TO BREAK YOUR HEART, OKAY?
RIGHT... OKAY?!
BEING SOMEONE'S SEX TOY IS ALL BUT MY SPECIALTY. STILL...WHY DO YOU NEED TO DO ALL OF THIS? COULDN'T YOU JUST DO IT WITH THIS ZATARIO GUY?
THAT'S-- IT'S NOT EASY FOR ME TO TALK ABOUT THIS. I'M ALMOST... INTIMIDATED.
HE'S BEAUTIFUL, HE'S SURELY SLEPT WITH MANY WOMEN. I DON'T WANT TO LOOK BAD.
AND I, WELL... NEED TO RELIEVE SOME STRESS.
AWESOME!
GREAT PLAN... BUT WHY ME?
THERE ARE DOZENS OF HOOKUP APPS--I'VE GOT THEM ALL--AND YOU'RE A REALLY PRETTY DEVIL.
...
I THOUGHT YOU HATED ME.
DID YOU... CHANGE YOUR MIND?

I WAS HORRIBLE LAST NIGHT. BUT YOU STILL CAME BY THIS MORNING TO SEE HOW I WAS. MAYBE YOU'RE TOO STUPID, OR TOO KIND. MAYBE BOTH...
BUT YOU'RE THE ONLY ONE IN THE OFFICE THAT DOESN'T HATE ME, EVEN AFTER SEEING ME AT MY WORST...I TRUST YOU. AND I NEVER TRUST ANYONE.
SWEET! THEN I'M IN! ♥
BUT ONLY IF YOU CANCEL THE RULE ABOUT DOGS.
GRRR...OKAY, FINE!
WELL, NOW THAT THAT'S ALL CLEAR... SHALL WE BEGIN?
CRACK
YES! ♥
PAT
PAT
ERM... WHERE DO WE START?
RELAX, LEAVE IT ALL TO ME.
FOR TONIGHT, LET'S JUST TAKE THINGS ONE STEP AT A TIME...
ARE...YOU SURE?
YES! AND THEN...
WEREN'T YOU INTERESTED IN SOME TECHNIQUE WITH A WEIRD NAME? YOU SEEMED PRETTY EXCITED ABOUT IT!
I FIGURE I OWE YOU ONE, RIGHT?
SBRILL
HE HE... ♥
OH, YES...

ZA'ATAR WILL LOSE HIS MIND WITH ME! ♥
THANKS TO THIS STUPID PENGUIN, I'LL BE GREAT AT THIS IN NO TIIIIIIME...
UH... ♥
UH...WHAT WAS I SAYING? I MEAN... I'LL GET MYSELF BACK ON TRACK, FINALLY GET MORE CONFIDENT, THEN MAYBE... WHA-WHAT?!
HOW CAN HE MOVE LIKE THA-THAT?
AND... WHA-WHAT WAS I SAYING? RIGHT, YES. THIS IS... IT'S...
UH... UHNN... ♥
OUUUFFFFFF!!!
...A NEW BEGINNING!

INFERNUM PRESS
SEE WHAT I MEAN?! THAT DAMN FOUR-EYES JUST GOT GROUP EDITOR!
TO THINK SHE'S ONLY HERE BECAUSE SHE COULDN'T HACK IT AS A WRITER...
SHE USED TO BRING THE COFFEE! AND NOW... THIS!
IT'S NOT SUCH A SURPRISE. HAVE YOU SEEN HER?
DIAVOLINO
QUIET, RESERVED, PRETTY...PLUS THOSE TINY SKIRTS OF HERS.
SHE ACTS SHY, BUT IT'S OBVIOUS SHE GAVE HIS GREAT DARKNESS THE PUPPY DOG EYES.
SHE'S THAT KIND OF DEVIL. GOT TO BE.
YOU THINK? ISN'T HIS GREAT DARKNESS GAY?
WHO KNOWS? I SAY HE'S BEEN SEDUCED.
WE BETTER STOP. PAPRIKA COULD HEAR US.
DIAVOLINO
HER? SHE'S TOO BUSY PRETENDING TO WORK.
SHE DOESN'T EVEN TAKE A COFFEE BREAK LIKE NORMAL PEOPLE...
...ALL SO HIS GREAT DARKNESS WILL COMPLIMENT HER JUST A LITTLE BIT MORE!
THAT'S THE ONLY WAY SHE CAN GET AHEAD IN PUBLISHING.
ESPECIALLY IF SHE CAN'T FIND HERSELF A BESTSELLER SOON...
HE HE HE!
NEW
SHUT YOUR HOLES, WORMS!

SOME--SOMETHING WRONG, PAPRIKA?
IT--IT WAS JUST A JOKE--
NO!
THAT'S LAST OF MY PATIENCE!
PAT...IENCE?
THIS...THIS INSULT WILL NOT STAND...
IT CAN'T GO UNPUNISHED!
DIAVOLON FAN
AND WHILE I'M CONSIDERING HIS PENANCE...
ONE OF YOU! GO TO MY EX'S HOUSE AND BRING ME HIS SORRY ASS.
IMMEDIATELY!
I'M TALKING YESTERDAY!
WHAT?! SHE'S--
SHUT UP!
LOUIS DIAVOLON FAN
HAVE YOU SEEN HER?
SHE'S NOT HERSELF.
WHATEVER HAPPENED, SHE'S WAY ANGRIER THAN USUAL!
WHA--WHAT SHOULD WE DO?
WHATEVER THE HELL SHE SAYS. UNTIL SHE'S OVER THIS.
AND...HOW LONG IS THAT GOING TO TAKE?
SPICE IT UP
-BURNET
PITCH
PAGE 21

CHAPTER 5

I PLAN TO ENJOY MYSELF HERE!

A FEW YEARS LATER...
WHERE ARE THE COVERS? THEY'RE SUPPOSED TO BE READY FOR APPROVAL!
YOU'RE ASKING ME?
INFERNUM PRESS
BEEEP
BEEEP
YOU WERE ASSIGNED THE NEW BOOK'S COVER AS WELL AS THE REPRINT!
I CAN'T FIND THE FILES!
BEEEP
TIME'S UP!
PAPRIKA WILL BE HERE IN SECONDS!
SHE SAID SHE WANTED THIS STUFF APPROVED BEFORE LUNCH.
IF THEY'RE NOT READY WHEN SHE GETS HERE... WE'RE DEAD!
PLAN
I WANT YOU TO WORK
COVERS
RUE?! WHERE IS RUE?
WHY ISN'T SHE HELPING?
SLOWLY, SLOWLY... THERE WE GO...
24K GOLD LEAF FOR HER LICORICE GINGER TEA. AND IT HAS TO BE FLOATING.
MISS PAPRIKA WILL NOT ACCEPT OTHERWISE!
FLOATING... A PEACEFUL LEAF...
NOT SUBMERGED... NOT DROWNING...
NOT...

LET'S GO, RUE!
QUIT PLAYING AROUND AND HELP US WITH OUR PROBLEMS, ALREADY!
STUMP
CRASH
WHAT THE HELL, ANISETTE!
I'M NOT A SECRETARY ANYMORE! I'M THE C.C.O.'S PERSONAL ASSISTANT!
SHE'S GOT EXCLUSIVE RIGHTS ON BULLYING ME!
UFF...
YOU REALLY HAVE JOINED THE ENEMY...
WHAT DO YOU MEAN?
NORI + RUE
WHATEVER. I'M BEYOND BUSY. IT'S BEEN DAYS SINCE MY LAST QUICKIE... AND NOW?
YOU SHOULDN'T TALK ABOUT SEX AT WORK...
THAT SPECIAL DELIVERY FUCKBOY FROM HEAVEN'S EXPRESS IS TEMPORARILY IN AN EXCLUSIVE RELATIONSHIP... THANKS TO SOME "PROJECT."
"TEMPORARILY EXCLUSIVE"?
"PROJECT"?
DOES DILL EVEN KNOW WHAT THOSE WORDS MEAN?
MAYBE THEY DREW HIM A DIAGRAM.
BUT MORE THAN THAT, I WONDER...
...WHAT SCHEMING VILLAIN LOCKED HIM DOWN--
HEAVEN EXPRE
HERE I AAAAAM~~!!!

HOW ARE YOU, MY OBEDIENT LITTLE--
EHRM
--COLLEAGUES! OR, OR EVEN FRIENDS! THAT'S WHAT I MEANT!
GOOD MORNINGGG~~!!!
WELCOME BACK TO MY HEADSPACE.
EVERYONE GOOD? YOU MISSED ME, RIGHT?
BLINK ONCE FOR "YES," OR NOT AT ALL.
GOOD! NOW BACK TO ME.
THAT ANGRY, PETTY, UNSYMPATHETIC MISS PAPRIKA IS NO MORE!
EMPORIO MIRKA
LOOK AT THIS! THEY'RE PAYING ATTENTION! STARING BACK AT ME WITH THOSE BEADY LITTLE MIDDLE MANAGEMENT EYES!
I'M RELAXED, I DRESS AS I PLEASE, I'M DEVILISHLY CHARISMATIC...AND SEXY, OF COURSE!
IT'S GOING TO BE A REAL BURDEN, BEING PRODUCTIVE WHILE ALL THESE GUYS DROOL OVER ME...
...

WE...WE DON'T HAVE THE COVER DESIGNS READY FOR YOUR MAGNANIMOUS APPROVAL.
BUT WE'RE SORRY!
WE HUMBLY BEG YOUR FORGIVENESS! MAYBE YOU COULD REVIEW THIS IN THE MEANTIME?
...
OF COURSE! HOW COULD I FORGET?!
THE CLASS HOTTIE NEVER GETS NOTICED UNTIL SHE LETS HER HAIR DOWN AND TAKES OFF HER GLASSES!
IT'S ONLY THEN THAT HER SEX APPEAL CAN SHATTER THE HEARTS OF HER CLASSMATES (AND THE PEOPLE WATCHING AT HOME).
SBRILL SBRILL
WINK WINK
MHHH...
ADORE ME, NOW! SHOWER ME WITH YOUR APPROVAL!
IS... EVERYTHING OKAY?
DO--DO YOU NEED A TOOTHPICK, MISS PAPRIKA?
HEAVEN'S EXPRESS
SHIT. LOOKS LIKE THEY'RE THE SAME AS EVER.
BUT ME?

I FOUND OUT MY FATHER'S LIES WERE LONGER THAN HIS HORNS. HE LIED TO MY MOM. TO ME.
WAS HE ALWAYS LYING? NO IDEA. THAT ASSHOLE'S HIDING IN ITALY AND WON'T RETURN MY CALLS.
WHAT REPLIES I DO GET ARE JUST VERSIONS OF THE SAME: "NONE OF YOUR BUSINESS" OR "IT'S MY PROBLEM NOT YOURS" OR, MY FAVORITE... "MEN HAVE URGES YOU CAN'T UNDERSTAND."
BUT HE DOES NOT UNDERSTAND MINE! OVER AND OVER, HE TOLD ME TO BE A MILD-MANNERED WOMAN. HE SILENCED MY URGES. SHAME HE COULDN'T SILENCE HIS OWN. TALK ABOUT A DOUBLE STANDARD.
MY FATHER! THE STATE'S MOST CONSERVATIVE JUDGE, WHO HAD A HEART ATTACK SNIFFING COKE AT AN ORGY.
ALL WHILE SHAMING ME FOR A LOW-CUT SHIRT.
DAD
Fucking hypocrite! You can't ignore me forever! How long has this been going on?
That's none of your business.
Bullshit! I want answers...
TSK! ENJOY ITALY, DAD.
BECAUSE I PLAN TO ENJOY MYSELF HERE! THERE'S A LOT TO CATCH UP ON.
AND NOT A MOMENT TOO SOON... BECAUSE I MET SOMEONE! ♥

ZA'ATAR, THE EXECUTIVE PRODUCER FOR THE UPCOMING MOVIE BASED ON OUR BESTSELLER SPICE IT UP!
HE'S ALWAYS ARGUING WITH HIS GREAT DARKNESS ABOUT SOME STUPID GRANULAR DETAIL. HE'S MERCILESS ON THE JOB AND DOES WHATEVER IT TAKES TO GET WHAT HE WANTS...SO BASICALLY, HE'S FLAWLESS.
WE'VE ONLY MET ONCE, BUT I KNOW ALL I NEED TO KNOW ABOUT HIM.
HE'S EDUCATED, CHARMING, AND OF COURSE... SEXY AS HELL...
OKAY. SO I'M CRUSHING LIKE A HIGH SCHOOLER.
TIME'S UP, I KNOW.
UNTIL I SEE HIM AGAIN, IT'LL BE HARD TO FOCUS ON WORK...LIKE RIGHT NOW! ARGH! ♥
WHY DOES MY IMAGINATION MUSCLE HAVE TO BE SO HUNGRY TO FLEX?! ♥
BUT WHO AM I KIDDING? I LOVE A GOOD FANTASY... ♥
SBRILL
MISS PAPRIKA...

ANF!
ANF!
ANF!
ANF!
YOU'VE REALLY DEVELOPED A TASTE FOR THIS!
ANF!
THE BATHROOM, THE DRESSING ROOM... THE ROCKS BY A CROWDED BEACH... AND YESTERDAY! BEHIND THE BUSHES! AND NOW? THE OFFICE BROOM CLOSET!
EVERYWHERE BESIDES THE BEDROOM! EVERYWHERE WE MIGHT GET CAUGHT!
WE'VE FOUND OURSELVES QUITE THE KINK, HAVEN'T WE?
AH...AHHHH! T-THAT'S NOT TRUEEEEWWH...
EHM... MISS?
IS ALL GOOD?
...OR MAYBE IT IS...JUST A LITTLEE...

AGH! WHA-- WHAT?
EHM... EVERYONE ELSE LEFT A FEW MINUTES AGO.
I THINK MAYBE YOU DOZED OFF?
I CAN'T BELIEVE IT! IT MUST BE A GLITCH IN THE TIMESTREAM...OR I JUST GOT LOST IN MY FANTASY.
OH, BEELZEBUB!
I'M SO SORRY! I WAS LOST IN MY THOUGHTS FOR A SECOND THERE.
NO NEED TO EXPLAIN! I GET IT. THESE MEETINGS ARE EXHAUSTING.
PLUS, THERE'S ALL THIS FUSS ABOUT THE MOVIE...
YEAH. I CAN'T WAIT FOR THE MARKET! HOPEFULLY IT'LL GIVE ME A CHANCE TO RELAX!
BESIDES ALL THE WORK MEETINGS OF COURSE...
I COULDN'T AGREE MORE! I'M COUNTING THE DAYS! BUT NOT FOR THE MARKET, TO BE HONEST...
OH...YEAH? FOR--FOR WHAT, THEN?
ITALY!
SOMEWHERE NEW! WITH NEW PLACES, NEW FLAVORS...
AND AT LAST...
...A CHANCE TO GET TO KNOW EACH OTHER.
AWAY FROM WORK, I MEAN!
MAYBE HAVE A FEW DRINKS TOGETHER...
I KNOW A VERY GOOD PIZZERIA THAT...

OTHERWISE, WE...WE CAN...
!
GNAK
BEAN!
WHAT THE FUUUUUUUUUUUUCK
SOMEBODY HELP MEEE!!!
GET THIS DAMN PLUSH OFF ME BEFORE I THROW BOTH OF YOU OUT THE WINDOW, YOU FUCKING DELIVERY BOY!
OH, NO!
I--I'M SO SORRY!
SHE ALWAYS GETS A BIT HYPERACTIVE AFTER SHE EATS HER ENERGIZING CROQUETTES!
THIS IS THE THIRD TIME THIS WEEK! ENOUGH, ALREADY!
WHAT...AM I SEEING HERE?
FUCK.
OKAY, SO... LET ME EXPLAIN.

HOW CAN I SAY THIS ELEGANTLY?
IT'S NOT WHAT IT LOOKS LIKE.
THERE'S NOTHING GOING ON WITH US...EXCEPT FOR THIS.
IT'S JUST PRACTICE.
I'M GOING TO NEED TO MEET ZA'ATAR STANDARDS. AND RIGHT NOW... I'M NO GOOD BETWEEN THE SHEETS.
BESIDES NOT HAVING DONE IT FOR HALF A CENTURY, LIKE...
Z
I KNOW IT'S BIZARRE, BUT I WANT TO IMPRESS HIM.
AND ANYWAY, DILL'S BIZARRE TOO. HE'S JUST AS FINE WITH OUR ARRANGEMENT AS I AM. I'LL BE AN EXPERT BY THE END.
BUT PROGRESS HAS BEEN SLOW GOING. WELL, THAT'S IF THOSE MULTIPLE ORGASMS DON'T COUNT.
YOU KNOW WHAT? CONSIDERING HOW LITTLE I FELT BEFORE, THEY DO!
I KNOW I'LL HAVE TO BE MORE PROACTIVE EVENTUALLY, AND I WANT TO, I SWEAR...
BUT FIRST THINGS FIRST. THERE'S NO RUSH. I'M TAKING MY TIME!
ANYWAY, WHERE WERE WE?

OH, YOU MUST BE ZATARIO!
I'M DILL AND THIS CUTIE IS BEAN.
I'M JUST A HUMBLE COURIER AT HEAVEN'S EXPRESS.
NOT TO MENTION A FAVORITE AMONG THE LADIES OF INFERNUM PRESS.
WOOF!
HEAVEN'S EXPRESS
IT'S "ZA'ATAR."
AND WHAT DO YOU MEAN BY...
"FAVORITE"?!
CRACK
SIMPLE! HE'S THE ONLY ONE WHO DELIVERS THINGS INTACT... YOU KNOW HOW MUCH TAMPAX COST THESE DAYS?!
IT'S SIMPLE, I JUST--
AHAHAHAH!
HE'S LIKE...A LOCAL HERO!
I...SEE. THAT'S QUITE IMPORTANT, I SUPPOSE...
?
AND ABOUT THAT, I THINK I FEEL MY PERIOD HITTING... RIGHT NOW! I BETTER GO!
TALK TO YOU SOON, ZA'ATAR...

YOU FUCKING IDIOT!
YOU WERE JUST GOING TO TELL HIM YOU'RE SLEEPING WITH EVERYONE?
WELL...I'M AN HONEST GUY.
THERE'S NOTHING WRONG WITH THAT.
I THINK YOU SHOULD BE HONEST TOO...WITH ZATARIO.
WOW! YEAH! WHY DIDN'T I THINK OF THAT?
LET ME JUST CALL HIM BACK! "HEY! I LIKE YOU BUT I'M FUCKING THE DELIVERY BOY BECAUSE I'M AN AMATEUR IN THE SACK THAT WANTS TO GET BETTER FOR YOU!"
I DIDN'T MEAN TO UPSET YOU.
I GUESS YOU WANT TO SKIP TONIGHT'S SESSION?
DAMN IT! THAT'S LITERALLY WHAT'S HAPPENING--SHIT!
WELL, I DIDN'T SAY THAT...
I KNEW IT.
SHUT UP.
HEAVEN'S EXPRESS
I SHOULD TELL MY DAD I'LL BE HOME LATE, HE'LL WORRY.
FINE! WHATEVER.
JUST MOVE, DUDE.
MH...

RINGIRINGIRINGI
YOUR PHONE, PICKLE...
MM...IT'S MY SON, SAYING HE'LL BE LATE... AGAIN.
WHY WORRY? YOU SHOULD JUST BE HAPPY HE'S ENJOYING HIMSELF.
THE THING IS...HE'S ONLY BEEN SEEING ONE GIRL LATELY.
I DON'T LIKE IT. THAT'S NOT LIKE HIM.
USUALLY, HE'D BE INTERRUPTING US BY NOW. AND YOU'D BE CRUSHING ON HIM AND HIS BICEPS.
END OF THE STORY.
HA HA!
YOU THINK YOU'RE A JOKER, EH?
PFFF... NOT RIGHT NOW.
YOU KNOW WHAT, PICKLE?
I'LL GO HAVE A BETTER TIME WITH SOMEONE ELSE.
HEY MAN, WANT TO TRY A HOT DOG?
UH?
I DON'T LIKE SEEING PEOPLE SAD.
I'VE BEEN THERE MYSELF...
...UNTIL SOMETHING HAPPENED! I FOUND MY TRUE PLACE IN THE WORLD, SELLING HOT DOGS.
THAT, AND I REALIZED YOU SHOULD ALWAYS BACK UP YOUR VIDEOS ON THE CLOUD.
HOT
THANKS, MAN.
GNAM
BUT COME ON...
EVERYBODY KNOWS YOU'VE GOT TO BACK UP YOUR SHIT.
SIGH!

!
THIS HOT DOG SUUUUCKS!
WHY DON'T WE GET A LITTLE MORE COMFORTABLE, THEN HEAD TO THE BEDROOM? ♥
NO! I TOLD YOU! THE RULES!
NO KISSING! AND THE BED...
...IS OFF-LIMITS!
WOOF!
ARF
WOOF!
ARF
ARF
AH!
YEAH... THAT'S GOOOD...
CALL ME MISS PAPRIKA!
AND LOOK ME IN THE EYES WHEN YOU SAY IT.
NOPE
HUH?
LIKE ZATARIO...?
FINE, IF IT WORKS FOR YOU...
DO YOU LIKE THAT, "MISS PAPRIKA"?
YESS... ♥
HELL YES!
AND HOW ABOUT...SOME RECIPROCITY?
YOU KNOW, LIKE LETTING ME IN, FOR ONCE...
I BROUGHT CONDOMS, AND--
MAYBE TOMORROW, OKAY?

...I LIKE DOING THIS WITH YOU, BUT... WE'VE BEEN AT IT FOR A WHILE... AND WE'RE GOING NOWHERE.
WE NEED TO TALK.
!
BLOB BLOB
YOU THINK IT'S APPROPRIATE TO PUT THOSE FUCKING SUNGLASSES ON RIGHT NOW?
OF COURSE, THEY LOOK HOT ON ME!
WINK WINK
LIKE I WAS SAYING...
... YOU KEEP SAYING "TOMORROW." OR THAT OUR DEAL IS IMPORTANT.
BUT YOU'RE NEVER GOING TO GET BETTER IN BED IF YOU JUST KEEP RECEIVING.
COULD IT BE, THAT =EHM= MAYBE... YOU'RE A VIRGIN?
ARE THOSE YOUR LAST WORDS!?
I'VE HAD PLENTY OF--WELL, I'VE HAD SOME-- I'VE HAD A BOYFRIEND
RIGHT, SURE...
...SEVEN YEARS AGO.
SO WHAT?
YOU MIGHT HAVE NOTICED I'M NOT THE WORLD'S BIGGEST PERSON...
SLOW DOWN, SLOW DOWN!
I WASN'T JUDGING... I WAS JUST SURPRISED!
WHY DON'T YOU START BY TELLING ME WHAT YOU LIKED DOING WITH YOUR EX?
LET'S START FROM THERE...
HEY! WOULD YOU LIKE IT IF I ASKED YOU SOMETHING LIKE THAT?
ABSOLUTELY NOT! AND YET...
I--I DON'T KNOW HOW TO ANSWER, OKAY? WE WERE BOTH REALLY YOUNG AND WE ONLY DID WHAT HE LIKED. AND ALSO, IT SOUNDS STUPID, BUT...
I FELT GUILTY EVERY TIME.
I WAS... VERY CONFUSED.

I... NEEDED PHYSICAL CONTACT, NEEDED TO FEEL CLOSE TO SOMEONE... THAT'S WHY IT TOOK ME SO LONG TO REALIZE I WAS SUFFERING. HE DIDN'T CARE ABOUT ME.
WHEN MY MOTHER HELPED ME SEE THAT, ALMOST EVERYTHING CHANGED... I THOUGHT MY FATHER WAS RIGHT, THAT I WAS ONLY DATING BECAUSE I WAS EASY, HOOKING UP WITH THE FIRST GUY I MET.
IN THE END, I LIVED TO MEET HIS EXPECTATIONS. WHEN I CALLED YOU A FEW DAYS AGO, I REALIZED IT WAS TIME TO TAKE WHAT I WANT AND BE MYSELF.
I WANT ZA'ATAR...I WANT A HEALTHY, SATISFYING RELATIONSHIP. AND I NEED YOUR HELP TO GET IT!
WAIT! WHY AM I ADMITTING THESE THINGS? HE'LL THINK I'M CRAZY...
THAT WAS MORE OF AN OUTBURST THAN AN ANSWER...
SEE?! I WAS RIGHT. I RUINED EVERYTHING!
...BUT IT'S COOL YOU OPENED UP TO ME! ♥
THAT MEANS WE'RE SUPER-FRIENDS NOW!
SUPER-FRIENDS-WITH-BENEFITS! ♥
WHAT? DON'T GET AHEAD OF YOURSELF, BUDDY!
YOU'RE STILL JUST A WALKING, TALKING SEX TOY.
WITH SWEET SHADES!
MAYBE, AS DILL-DO... YOU COULD...
...
YOU HAD IT WITH YOU, READY TO GO?
YES! ♥

GOOD EVENING!
HELLO... IS PAPRIKA HOME?
I'D LIKE TO SURPRISE HER...
WHY YES, SHE IS!
I CAN'T BELIEVE IT...
IT'S FINALLY HAPPENING!
YOU'RE TOTALLY SURE?
BUT NOT ON THE BED?
ASK AGAIN AND I'LL PUNCH YOU!
NOT ON THE BED.
SO, THAT'S IT THEN! WATCH OUT, BABY...
...HERE I COME! ♥
"BABY"?
HEY! I WAS GOING FOR ATMOSPHERE!
TLACK
SWEETIE?

I'M IN--♥
HEY, SWEETIE! I HOPE I'M NOT DISTURB--
--FINALLY!
OH! I...WELL, GOOD EVENING, MA'AM!
...
WHAT THE--
AAAAAAAAAAAA
HMM?
I-I THINK I HEARD MISS PAPRIKA'S VOICE!
WHAT? HOW?! WE'RE TWO STATES APART!

WHY DON'T YOU JOIN US, ZA'ATAR?
MY FRIENDS ARE WAY MORE FUN THAN THAT UPTIGHT LITTLE DEVIL...
DON'T TALK LIKE THAT ABOUT MISS PAPRIKA, BURNET!
YOU HAVE YOUR FUN...I'M NOT THAT KIND OF PERSON, AND NEITHER IS SHE...I THINK... I HOPE...
YOU CAN BET SHE IS NOT!
DO...YOU KNOW THIS DILL GUY?
BILL? NEVER HEARD OF HIM...
BUT IF YOU WEREN'T UP FOR FUN, YOU SHOULDN'T HAVE COME HERE.
I CAME HERE TO DO WORK. YOU KNOW, CASTING. FOR OUR MOVIE...
I DON'T KNOW IF IT'S THE STRESS OF THE PRODUCTION, OR WHAT...
...BUT IT SEEMS LIKE YOU'RE JEALOUS OF MISS PAPRIKA.
COME ON, LEAVE HIM...
MISTER WORKY WORK JUST HATES FUN...
HAVE A GOOD NIGHT! DON'T PULL A MUSCLE...

SOME HELP YOU WERE BACK THERE...
GO HOME. OR STAY AND ENTERTAIN EACH OTHER...
I DON'T CARE.
DID...I MISS SOMETHING?
?
PAPRIKA, PAPRIKA...
GLUG
THIS SPELL YOU'VE PUT ON ZA'ATAR...
JUST WHEN I THOUGHT IT WAS SETTLED BETWEEN US...
"I WAS SURE A NASTY LITTLE WORKAHOLIC LIKE YOU...NO FRIENDS, NO SOCIAL SKILLS... WAS ENSURED A LONELY FUTURE...
"BUT NOW MY FRIEND, ZA'ATAR'S GOT IT BAD FOR YOU! LIKE A DAMN TEENAGER!
"IT'S SO OBVIOUS HE WANTS YOU. AND HE ALWAYS GETS WHAT HE WANTS..."

CRASH
MOTHERFUCKER!
THERE'S NO TWO WAYS ABOUT IT. I'LL HAVE TO FIGHT TOO.
AND I WILL GET WHAT I WANT.
HELLO? I'D LIKE TO BOOK A FLIGHT.
HOW FAST CAN YOU GET ME TO NEW YORK?
FIRST CLASS, OF COURSE...

CHAPTER 6

YOU WERE THE ONE SURPRISING ME!

WAKEY WAKEY, SLEEPYHEAD.
SOMEBODY GOT HOME LATE LAST NIGHT...
THE USUAL CASANOUWA-- CASANOV-- WHATEVER HIS NAME WAS!
AHR AHR!
BUT SPEAKING OF THE USUAL...
...LET'S FORGET IT! HOW ABOUT A SPECIAL BREAKFAST? PIZZA, EGGS, A LITTLE MILK...
NOW, I KNOW WHAT YOU'RE THINKING...WHY'S HE BEING SO NICE? IS IT CHRISTMAS?
FZZz
FZZz
BUT THESE DAYS, WE ONLY SPEND TIME TOGETHER AT WORK OR BREAKFAST, SO I THOUGHT...WHY NOT MAKE THAT TIME SPECIAL?
TODAY, WE CAN FINALLY RELAX!
HOW'S THAT SOUND, DILL?
HELLO?
BEWARE OF THE BEAN!
BEST
CHIPS
I GET WANTING YOUR BREAKFAST IN BED, BUT--

DRIIIN
DADDY! ♥
YES, SORRY! I SLEPT AT PAPRIKA'S!
IT WAS GETTING LATE, I FIGURED YOU WERE SLEEPING, OR MAYBE DOING SOMETHING BETTER... HE HE! ♥
HOW'D YOUR DATE GO?
MY WHAT? IT...WENT FINE...
NO, NO, YOU'RE NOT BOTHERING...
I'M JUST HAVING A QUICK BREAKFAST =SNIFF= THE FIRST THING I FOUND IN THE FRIDGE.
REMEMBER TO EAT, OKAY? I DON'T WANT YOU STARVING IN THAT CHIC HOUSE OF HERS.
DON'T WORRY! PEPPER-- THAT'S PAPRIKA'S MOM-- INSISTED ON COOKING US SOME HIGHLY CALORIC DELIGHT. SHE SAID HER DAUGHTER LOOKED A LITTLE THIN.
HER MOM?!
THIS THING'S THAT SERIOUS?!
HA! NO. IT'S A LONG STORY.
FOR LATER.
WHEN I'M LESS BUSY.
ANGELS GONNA
BUSY? DO-DOING WHAT?
THE THING IS, PAPRIKA'S HOUSE IS SO LUXURIOUS! YOU CAN'T IMAGINE THE FEATURES SHE'S INSTALLED. SHE'S EVEN GOT A BATHROOM JUST FOR HER BEDROOM!
WOW...
YEAH, I MEAN... IT'S LIKE SCIENCE FICTION OVER HERE!
YOU'LL NEVER GUESS WHAT I'M DOING WITH BEAN RIGHT NOW!
HIGH-CLASS DOGGY STUFF! ♥

WHAT THE FUCK...
WOAAAARF!
YOU ARE USING MY BIDET...
TO WASH THAT... FILTHY BEAST OF YOURS?!
"BIDET"? IS THAT FRENCH FOR PUPPY BATHTUB?
SOUNDS LIKE I NEED ONE OF MY OWN!
NO, YOU IDIOT!
EVERYONE'S GOT A BIDET IN ITALY. IT'S FOR WASHING YOUR JUNK!
ISN'T... SHOWERING ENOUGH?
IT'S NOT ENOUGH!
IF YOU CAN USE IT TO WASH YOUR PUSSY, WHY CAN'T I USE IT ON MY PUPPY?
IT EVEN RHYMES!
THAT'S NOT WHAT RHYMING IS!
I...HAVE SO MUCH TO EXPLAIN.
WOSH
LIKE WHY MY MOTHER'S MAKING BREAKFAST.
SURE, I COULD CATCH YOU UP...
...BUT MAYBE IT'S EASIER TO JUST SHOW YOU.
BREAKFAST IS SERVED!

AAAAAAAAY
DON'T WORRY, PAPRIKA!
I--I'LL JUST WAIT UNTIL YOU'RE FINISHED IN THERE...
...IF YOU EVER ANSWERED MY CALLS, YOU'D KNOW THAT BERRY TOOK THE KIDS TO THEIR AUNT'S AND WILL BE GONE FOR A COUPLE OF DAYS. I THOUGHT I'D VISIT AS A SURPRISE, SPEND SOME TIME TOGETHER. BUT...
YOU WERE THE ONE SURPRISING ME! HE HE HE!
OPEN YOUR MOUTH, BIG BOY...
AAAHM...
I'M GOING TO THROW UP. HERE IT COMES...
THAT'S... GOOD!
TRY ANOTHER BITE OF LASAGN--YARGH, I MEAN--OF THIS HANDMADE, LOW-CARB PASTA WITH TOMATO ESSENCE AND ORGANIC MEATS. I WANT YOU STRONG AND HEALTHY FOR PAPRIKA!
WOW! THOSE BICEPS!
STRIZZ
I THINK IT'S TIME FOR BED, MOTHER.
YOU'VE INVADED OUR PRIVACY ENOUGH FOR ONE NIGHT.
ALREADY?
BUT I WANT TO KNOW EVERYTHING!
I NEED DETAILS!
MUNCH
MUNCH
WHERE, WHEN, WHY...
...AND HOW LONG HAVE YOU TWO BEEN DATING?
DATING? WE'RE NOT--
SPLAT
IT'S ALL PRETTY NEW...HE HE HE HE!

EITHER PLAY ALONG OR SHUT UP. YOU THINK I'D EVER TELL MY MOTHER YOU'RE JUST A WINGED SEX TOY?
BUT--
SINCE WE'RE FRIENDS, I'LL HELP...BY TELLING HER MY OWN VERSION OF THE TRUTH.
TRUST ME!
I'M A COURIER AT HEAVEN'S EXPRESS. WE'VE KNOWN EACH OTHER FOR YEARS, SINCE I'M ALWAYS DELIVERING STUFF TO PAPRIKA'S OFFICE, BUT...THINGS HAVE BEEN DIFFERENT FOR THE PAST WEEK.
HOW CUTE! YOU'RE JUST GETTING STARTED...
THE BEST PART, HE HE! ♥
WELL, THEN LET ME TELL YOU...
...PAPRIKA HAS SUFFERED FOR TOO LONG.
AND I'VE GOT A BIG, STRONG HORN RIGHT HERE...WHICH I'LL USE TO WHOOP YOUR BEAUTIFUL ASS IF NECESSARY, GOT IT?
DON'T BELIEVE ME? ASK PAPRIKA'S SCOUNDREL OF AN EX.
I ALREADY KILLED ONE TOXIC WEDDING, I CAN DO IT AGAIN.
WOW!
I THINK I'VE GOT A CRUSH ON YOUR MOM, NOW... ♥
!
MOOOOOM! YOU'RE ALWAYS SO DRAMATIC! DON'T LISTEN TO HER, DILL. REALLY.
I THINK IT'S SWEET.
I PROMISE YOU, YOU SWEET, SEXY LASAGNA CHEF, THAT I'LL MAKE YOUR DAUGHTER VERY HAPPY.
KILL ME NOW.

YOU TWO LOVEBIRDS CAN GO, I'LL TAKE THE GUEST ROOM! TOMORROW, I'LL MAKE YOU SOUFFLÉ PANCAKES... YOU'RE TOO THIN, PAPRIKA! ♥
I AM NOT!
AND ANYWAY, DILL WAS JUST LEAVING...
...BUT PANCAKES!
WHAT THE FU--
SO, YOUR MOM MENTIONED THAT EX OF YOURS...ACCORDING TO MY INTEL, HE MUST'VE BEEN A REAL JERK...
SUDDENLY YOU'RE THE CIA AND FBI ROLLED INTO ONE...
300 MAIL
I'M FINISHING SOME EMAILS AND GOING TO BED. I'D ADVISE YOU TO DO THE SAME...IN THE BATHTUB.
SO... NO BED TODAY?
NOT FOR YOU.
MY MOTHER'S ON THE OTHER SIDE OF THIS WALL, AND YOU'RE NOT ZA'ATAR. AND ONLY HE'S ALLOWED IN MY BED, YOU STUPID PENGUIN.
BUT I'M NOT SLEEPY YET! MAYBE WE CAN FIND A WAY TO TIRE OURSELVES OUT, HE HE HE!
WE'VE BARELY MADE PROGRESS! ♥
I'VE BEEN INSIDE YOU FOR LIKE THREE SECONDS AT MOST.
NOT TONIGHT! I'M NOT IN THE MOOD. FORGET IT.
THEN I'LL JUST TAKE A TOUR OF THIS ROOM... IT'S HUGE!
MY PLACE IS NOTHING LIKE THIS.
DO WHAT YOU WANT, AS LONG AS YOUR PENIS TOURS AWAY FROM ME.
THIS CLOSET'S BIG ENOUGH TO BE BEAN'S BEDROOM!
WHY IN HELL'S NAME ARE YOU WEARING MY STUFF?!
SO MANY BOOKS, WOW! YOU MUST REALLY LIKE READING! I MEAN, YOU DO WORK IN PUBLISHING...
BUT NOT EVEN ONE SINGLE COMIC BOOK?!
COMICS? WHO DO YOU THINK I AM?
WHAT'S THIS?
I SEE YOU'RE INTERESTED IN SOME...VERY SPECIFIC GENRES! WE'VE GOT THE SAME TASTE, YOU VICIOUS GIRL! ♥
SO? YOU READ COMIC BOOKS... WHICH I'M SURE ARE JUST THE USUAL PORN GARBAGE.
HELL YES THEY ARE! I DRAW THEM TOO, FOR FUN...

WAIT A SECOND-- I'VE READ THIS ONE, TOO!
WOW. YOU DO READ BOOKS WITHOUT PICTURES, RIGHT?
I SAID WE HAD SIMILAR TASTE!
THIS IS SO COOL!
SPICE IT UP! IS SO GOOD!
THAT BURNET'S A GENIUS.
BURNET
SPICE IT UP!
YOU PUBLISHED THIS, RIGHT? IT'S LIKE YOUR BEST SELLER, ISN'T IT?
WEREN'T YOU THE EDITOR ON IT, TOO? YOU HAD TO BE, I REMEMBER!
BY WHICH I MEAN I REMEMBER A GIRL AT INFERNUM TELLING ME WHEN WE WERE FLIRTING.
MH...
THIS STORY'S SO FULL OF ROMANCE AND SEX... SEX, SEX, SEX!
UMPF!
IT'S ALSO ABOUT A SEXUALLY FRUSTRATED YOUNG WOMAN, ABOUT THE BEAUTY IN DISCOVERING...
...HER BOOBS!
...WELL, YEAH. THOSE TOO.
I BET BURNET IS LIKE, THE COOLEST.
YOU SHOULD INTRODUCE ME TO HIM SOMEDAY!
...

I MEAN, WE'RE FRIENDS, AREN'T WE? SO, IF YOU WON'T PAY ME IN CUDDLING LIKE I'D LIKE, I THINK THIS IS THE LEAST YOU CAN DO. ♥
WHO KNOWS? MAYBE HE'LL SEE HOW SUPER FUNNY I AM AND WANT TO KEEP ME AROUND...
?
YOU WANT ME TO MAKE PROGRESS, RIGHT?
TO... RECIPROCATE?
YOU KNOW WHAT?
YOU-- YOU'RE RIGHT!
ANYTHING TO KEEP YOUR MOUTH SHUT!
Z-ZZIP

SBRILL
JUST THINK OF ME AS MISTER TATARRO!
TRUST ME. I ALWAYS AM.
AND BRACE YOURSELF, BECAUSE WHEN I RECIPROCATE, IT'S DOUBLE!
I CAN DO THIS, I CAN DO THIS...YEAH, I'VE DONE IT PLENTY OF TIMES!
WHAT'S THE MATTER?
IT'S... JUST BEEN A MINUTE SINCE I...
NEVER MIND! YOU'LL SEE! MY SUPER MACH 3 SUCKING TECHNIQUE WITH TURBO TONGUE!
IT... SOUNDS SORT OF ROUGH, MAYBE YOU SHOULD START A LITTLE SOFTER...
?
I'LL LEAVE YOU SO PLEASED YOU WON'T EVEN NEED IT ANYMORE!
THA-- THATS SOUNDS WORSE, ACTUALLY! BE GENTLE, PLEASE!
LISTEN, PAPRIKA. YOU DON'T EXACTLY SEEM... AT EASE, HERE...
IF YOU'RE NOT COMFORTABLE WITH THIS, IT'S NO PROBLEM.
IF YOU'RE NOT ENJOYING THIS TOO, THERE'S NO POINT!
I AM BEYOND AT EASE AND VERY EXCITED FOR THIS OPPORTUNITY, IS THAT CLEAR?
AAAAAAARGH!
I'M LYING. I'M TOTALLY TENSE.
SIGH.
PAPRIKA...
YOU'RE JUST GOING ABOUT THIS THE WRONG WAY.
...

OH YEAH? AND WHAT'S THE RIGHT WAY TO GO ABOUT IT, YOU SHIT FUCK ASS?
IT'S SIMPLE: LET ME HELP YOU.
WITH YOUR PERMISSION, I'LL GRAB YOUR HEAD AND...NO NEED TO THANK ME, BABY.
WOW, SUCH A GENTLEMAN!
JUST LET ME GIVE SOME FUCKING HEAD, BURNET!
CRACK!
WHAT DO YOU WANT FROM ME?
WE'RE IN YOUR MIND, AFTER ALL.
TAKE A LOOK...
SEE ANYTHING FAMILIAR?
DON'T TELL ME YOU THOUGHT SOME RANDOM GUY WOULD BE ENOUGH...
!
LOOK AT YOUR GUILT. IT'S ALWAYS THERE.
YOU WANT TO BE OBSCENE, BUT THE SECOND YOU GET A LITTLE DIRTY AND FLIRTY...YOU'RE UNCOMFORTABLE, RIGHT?
THE TRUTH, MY DEAR PAPPY...IS THAT YOU'LL ALWAYS BE DADDY'S LITTLE REPRESSED GIRL.
YOU'LL NEVER ENJOY SEX BECAUSE, YOU KNOW...YOU'LL ALWAYS BE WAITING FOR A PUSH.

TELL ME I'M WRONG.
!
OR DON'T, AND JUST KEEP TRYING IN VAIN...
YOU POOR, FRIGID LITTLE DEVIL!

SOFTER, OKAY? OTHERWISE-- YOU KNOW WHAT? DOESN'T MATTER.
WE'LL FIGURE THIS OUT SOME OTHER TIME, NO WORRIES. ♥
PAT PAT
YOU MUST REALLY THINK I'M STUPID!
PLONF
YOU THINK I DON'T KNOW?
YOU REALLY THINK I'M FRIGID! THAT I CAN'T DO THIS!
BUT I CAN! I'M PERFECTLY NORMAL!
I'M NOT THE PROBLEM!
YOU ARE!
...ME?
YOU'RE NOT MAKING ME COMFORTABLE!
YOU-- YOU'RE TOO WEIRD...TOO KIND... YOU'RE HIDING SOMETHING, YOU MUST BE!
NOW GO SLEEP IN THE BATHROOM BEFORE I REALLY GET PISSED OFF!
IF I DID SOMETHING TO BOTHER YOU... I'M SORRY, OKAY? REALLY SORRY.
GRR
YOU DON'T EVEN GET ANGRY IF I INSULT YOU?
YOU KNOW WHO NEVER GETS MAD? WHO'S ALWAYS SHINY AND SMILING?
MANIPULATIVE BASTARD ASSHOLES!
I...DON'T GET IT...
DROP THE ACT! TELL ME WHY YOU'RE DOING THIS!
IT CAN'T JUST BE ABOUT SEX... SO COME ON, OUT WITH IT!
...

LOOK, I NEVER LIE, SO I'LL JUST SAY...
IF YOU KNEW WHY I LIKE BEING AROUND YOU SO MUCH, YOU'D THINK I'M EVEN WEIRDER THAN YOU ALREADY DO.
SO...I WON'T TELL YOU. ♥
WHAT KIND...OF BULLSHIT ANSWER...IS THAT?!
YOU ARE SO INCREDIBLY...
...UNBEARABLE!
GOODNIGHT, THEN! ♥
AND IN THE MORNING... PANCAKES! ♥
SO...THAT'S HOW WE GOT HERE.
END OF STORY.
MY MOTHER FOUND US OUT AND WE... SURVIVED, SOMEHOW.
BUT WHAT IF IT WASN'T MY MOTHER? WHAT IF THE OFFICE CAUGHT US?
I CAN BARELY IMAGINE IT...
THE EMBARRASSMENT, THE SHAME... AND EVEN WORSE, PEOPLE MIGHT THINK DILL WAS MY... TSK...BOYFRIEND.
INFERNIUM PRESS
SO, RUE... RUETTE... LITTLE MISS RUE...
IT'S YOUR BFF ANISETTE, JUST WONDERING...
IS PAPRIKA SEEING SOMEONE? ♥

I SHOULDN'T **GOSSIP** ABOUT MISS PAPRIKA.
UMPF, COME ON!
IT'S NOT LIKE IT'S **NATIONAL SECURITY.**
IT'S SO **BORING** HERE! JUST GIVE ME **SOMETHING!** OR MAYBE YOU'RE JUST **ACTING** LIKE YOU KNOW SOMETHING...
WELL...I **DO** HANDLE ALL HER SCHEDULING, SO...
MISS PAPRIKA IS **VERY** PRECISE AND HABITUAL.
I THINK IF SHE'D MADE ANY **CHANGES** TO HER ROUTINE...**I'D NOTICE.**
MISS PAPRIKA CALENDAR
SLEEP
MEETING
VIDEO CALL
MEETING
DIAVOLINO NEW
DINNER WITH AUTHORS
MEETING DINNER
MEETING
BUT AS FAR AS **SPECULATING** GOES...I THINK MISS PAPRIKA IS INTO THAT **MISTER ZA'ATAR** AT **PURGATORY PICTURES.**
SHE **DID** MAKE ME **FORWARD** HER HIS **CALL** WHEN I COULD'VE HANDLED IT...
OH?
OF **COURSE,** ZA'ATAR! ♥
I **LOVE** TO PERSONALLY MICROMANAGE EVEN THE SMALLEST DETAILS OF MY **TAXES!**
FLAP
WHO DOESN'T?
I'VE **GOT** TO GET THIS ALL DOWN... ♥
ZAT + PAP
IS PAPRIKA **REALLY** CRUSHING THAT HARD?

COME ON, DILL...DON'T TELL ME YOU'RE STILL EXCLUSIVE!
DO NOT FLIRT WITH THIS GUY
WORK!
HEY!
SO, BIG BOY!
LET ME GUESS... IT'S SO HARD BEING "EXCLUSIVE," ISN'T IT?
WHY DON'T YOU COME CHAT WITH ME IN PRIVATE? WHO WOULD KNOW?
AND IF YOU BEHAVE... I'LL GIVE YOUR CAP BACK.
UNLESS YOU WANT TO TAKE IT YOURSELF, THAT IS! ♥
I-- WELL, I...
UH...
!
I'VE...GOT TO CALL YOU BACK. SOMETHING'S POPPED UP THAT REQUIRES MY IMMEDIATE ATTENTION.
GOODBYEEEEEEEEE! ♥
?!

THAT STUPID PENGUIN BETTER NOT BE PLAYING TRICKS ON ME! HE PROMISED!
NO EXTRA-CONTRACTUAL RELATIONS!
NOT AFTER HOW MUCH I SPENT ON GETTING HIM A FULL CHECKUP. SAFETY FIRST!
HEAVEN'S EXPRESS
YOU KNOW THAT THING ABOUT INDIRECT KISSING IF YOU ALL DRINK FROM THE SAME BOTTLE?
GRRR!
NEVER WILL I BE PENETRATED OR TOUCHED BY A PENIS THAT'S BEEN INSIDE ANISETTE OR ANYONE LIKE HER!
I DON'T WANT CRABS, ESPECIALLY ANISETTE'S!
I BET EVEN CONDOMS COULDN'T STOP THOSE!
WOF WOF WOF WOF!
MHHHHHH...
IT'S JUST SO GROSS!
JUST THINK OF ME...INDIRECTLY KISSING ANISETTE'S VAGINA! OR EVEN HER... YUCK...LIPS! HER CURSED TONGUE!
COULD ANYTHING BE MORE REVOLTING?
SLURP...
PCIU PCIU...
HAVE FUN
OKAY, ENOUGH FUCKING AROUND. TIME TO CATCH THE BASTARD RED-HANDED!
I KNEW THE WHOLE "I'M HONEST, HO HO HO!" THING WAS AN ACT.
HERE THEY ARE! NO DOUBT ANISETTE'S ALREADY GOT HER ASS IN THE...

MH...
THA-- THAT'S IT?
HE'S NOT VIOLATING THE CONTRACT... SO FAR.
KISSING IS STRICTLY FORBIDDEN BETWEEN US, SO THERE'S NO RISK OF INDIRECT SALIVA EXCHANGE WITH ANISETTE.
BUT STILL...
UH...
ANF!
ANF!
ANF!
ANF!
I FEEL... STRANGE...
WHY DOES THAT KISS SEEM SO MUCH BETTER...
...THAN ALL THE AWKWARD PASSES I'VE MADE ON HIM?
ANF!
ANF!
I ALSO... =UHHHHHH= I ALSO WANT THAT...
OUFFFFFFF!
!

WHAT? IT'S FINE...
ARE YOU KIDDING?
SOME PERVERT'S SPYING ON US!
WOF!
I HOPE THIS LECHER LIKES PAIN, 'CAUSE THERE'S A HELL OF A LOT OF IT COMING!
UH?!
SEE? NO ONE'S HERE!
SHIT.
I DON'T GET IT.
I KNOW I HEARD SOMETHING!
DAMN IT!
THIS IS THE MOST AGILITY I'VE EVER HAD, I SWEAR!

I'LL FIND THIS WEIRDO, WHOEVER HE WAS!
!
WOF! WOF! WOF!
I'D RECOGNIZE YOUR "OUFFF" ANYWHERE.
AS YOU CAN SEE, I STUCK TO OUR DEAL.
PLUS, I KEPT HER TOO BUSY TO ASK A MILLION INAPPROPRIATE QUESTIONS.
WHAT GOT YOU AROUSED? DOING THINGS IN PUBLIC, OR WAS IT THE KISSING?
IF YOU WANT A KISS, I'LL GIVE YOU ONE...AS SOON AS YOU COME DOWN.
WOF! WOF!
DOING THINGS IN PUBLIC?
DON'T EVEN JOKE ABOUT IT!
IF THIS WERE FICTION, WE'D HAVE TO PUT UP A MILLION DISCLAIMERS TELLING PEOPLE NOT TO DO THAT STUFF! IT'S ILLEGAL IN MANY STATES!
THAT'S SO SPECIFIC, AS SCOLDINGS GO...
LET'S GO! I'LL HELP YOU GET OFF!
HEAVEN'S EXPRESS
STAY BACK! YOU AND YOUR LIPS SOILED WITH ANISETTE'S BUSTY BACTERIA!
I CAN HANDLE MYSEAAAAAAAAAAARGH...
TUNF

YOU SHOULD STOP BEING SO ADORABLY AGGRESSIVE WITH PEOPLE WHO WANT TO HELP YOU.
AND BY THE WAY...
...I THINK I FIGURED OUT WHAT NEEDS TO BE DONE TO TURN YOU ON.
SO, I WAS THINKING... WHAT IF...
...WE WENT ON A DATE?

I'LL BE BACK SOON.
IF YOU'RE GOING TO LUNCH, CAN I JOIN?
I'M STARVING...
ERM, SORRY, BUT I'VE...GOT TO DINE ALONE TODAY.
WOOOSH
WOOOSH
YOU FIND ANYTHING OUT?

I THINK IT'S PAPRIKA AND THE COURIER...CAN YOU BELIEVE IT? HOW'D I DO?
GOOD. VERY GOOD!
WE'LL HAVE CONCRETE EVIDENCE SOON ENOUGH. AND WHEN WE DO...
...I'D KILL TO BE A FLY ON THE WALL WHEN POOR ZA'ATAR FINDS OUT.
WHO, JUST AS IT HAPPENS, IS KNOWN FOR HIS TEMPER...
THE CONTRACT BETWEEN INFERNUM PRESS AND PURGATORY PICTURES WILL BE DOOMED.
OR, AT LEAST, ZA'ATAR WILL MAKE SURE PAPRIKA'S DONE FOR.
AND THAT'S WHEN I TAKE HER PLACE. RIGHT, CUTIE?
BUT IF THE CONTRACT DOES FAIL...
...I'M COVERED. I'VE ALREADY RECEIVED A COMPETING PROPOSAL. AND IF I TAKE IT...
BURNET
SPICE IT UP!
AGREEMENT
...YOU'LL BE JOINING ME AND MY NICE, ROUND, DOLLAR-COVERED ASS.
TO BE CONTINUED...

MIRKA ANDOLFO

MIRKA ANDOLFO is an award-winning Italian artist and writer appreciated for her strong female characters.

She is considered a unique talent: her creator-owned books (***Unnatural***, ***Mercy***, ***Sweet Paprika***, ***Un/Sacred***) are published in more than 25 countries in the world (so far, the sales total more than 700,000 copies).

She has collaborated with DC Comics since 2015, working on titles including *Wonder Woman*, *Harley Quinn*, *DC Comics Bombshells*, *Punchline*, *Superman vs Lobo*. In 2020 she became the first Italian creator to work on both story and artwork at DC (*Harley Quinn Black + White + Red*).

Andolfo has also written for The Walt Disney Company, Marvel, Dynamite (*Red Sonja*), BOOM! Studios (*The Amazing World of Gumball*, *Buffy the Vampire Slayer*) and illustrated two issues of the award-winning *Ms. Marvel* series (Marvel).

As an illustrator, she's contributed to marketing and advertising campaigns for companies including Paramount, 20th Century Studios, Netflix, and Juventus, and has drawn comics and illustrations for many publishers both in Europe and in the United States.

"UNNATURAL is funny and sexy and smart and so many more things. But, most of all, it is a damning indictment of who we have been and who we continue to be as a society."
–The Oregonian
"A gorgeous fantasy erotica must-read."
–Geek.com
"A wonder to read and sure to become a classic."
–Outright Geekery
MIRKA ANDOLFO'S
UNNATURAL
"Beautiful to look at and a little scary to read, UNNATURAL is a great piece of writing that eerily mirrors today's world."
–AIPT
"Andolfo continues to craft a world that's both narratively and visually interesting, one that is clearly much more than what meets the eye."
–ComicBook.com

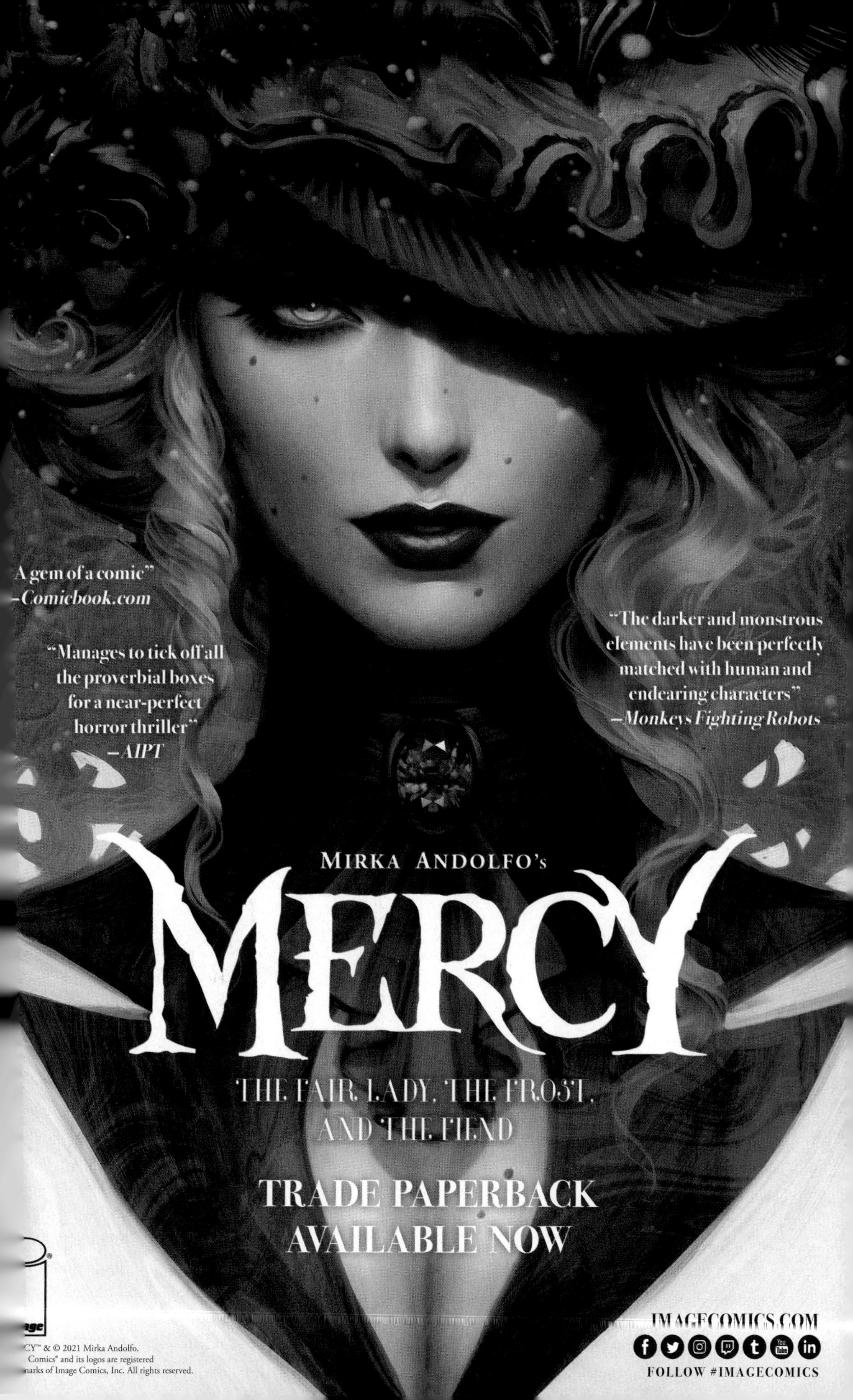

"A gem of a comic"
–Comicbook.com
"Manages to tick off all the proverbial boxes for a near-perfect horror thriller"
–AIPT
"The darker and monstrous elements have been perfectly matched with human and endearing characters"
–Monkeys Fighting Robots
MIRKA ANDOLFO's
MERCY
THE FAIR LADY, THE FROST, AND THE FIEND
TRADE PAPERBACK
AVAILABLE NOW
IMAGECOMICS.COM
FOLLOW #IMAGECOMICS

HE CAME TO THE U.S. FOR FORTUNE AND FREEDOM.
HE LEFT TO SAVE LIVES.
LEONE NOTES ON A LIFE
Carmine Di Giandomenico & Francesco Colafella
LEONE: NOTES ON A LIFE OGN
DECEMBER 2021
image
imagecomics.com #imagecomics
LEONE: NOTES ON A LIFE is ™ & © 2021 Carmine di Giandomenico & Francesco Colafella.
Image Comics® and its logos are registered trademarks of Image Comics, Inc. All rights reserved.

WE SHOULD DATE!
YOU SHOULD DIE!